"Do you want m[e]

Did she want him?
Impossible, preposterous, unnecessary
question. Of course she wanted him! She
yearned for him, *ached* for him. But…

And then suddenly she knew what was
wrong. "Do I want you?" Felicity managed,
a thread of near laughter running through
her words. "But who are you? I don't even
know your name. All I know is Rico—if in
fact that is the truth."

"The truth, *gatita?*" He laughed. "*Sí.* Oh,
yes, I told you the truth. My name really
is Rico—short for Ricardo. Ricardo Juan
Carlos Valeron at your service, *señorita.*"

The words pounded into her senses
like cruel blows, making her heart stop.
Ricardo Valeron. The one man who had
the power to make an appalling situation
even worse.

RED HOT REVENGE

The Hostage Bride
by
Kate Walker

There are times in a man's life...
when only seduction will settle old scores!

Pick up our exciting series of revenge-filled
romances—they're recommended and red-hot!

Kate Walker

THE HOSTAGE BRIDE

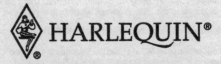

TORONTO • NEW YORK • LONDON
AMSTERDAM • PARIS • SYDNEY • HAMBURG
STOCKHOLM • ATHENS • TOKYO • MILAN • MADRID
PRAGUE • WARSAW • BUDAPEST • AUCKLAND

ISBN 0-373-12315-9

THE HOSTAGE BRIDE

First North American Publication 2003.

Copyright © 2001 by Kate Walker.

All rights reserved. Except for use in any review, the reproduction or
utilization of this work in whole or in part in any form by any electronic,
mechanical or other means, now known or hereafter invented, including
xerography, photocopying and recording, or in any information storage
or retrieval system, is forbidden without the written permission of the
publisher, Harlequin Enterprises Limited, 225 Duncan Mill Road,
Don Mills, Ontario, Canada M3B 3K9.

All characters in this book have no existence outside the imagination of
the author and have no relation whatsoever to anyone bearing the same
name or names. They are not even distantly inspired by any individual
known or unknown to the author, and all incidents are pure invention.

This edition published by arrangement with Harlequin Books S.A.

® and TM are trademarks of the publisher. Trademarks indicated with
® are registered in the United States Patent and Trademark Office, the
Canadian Trade Marks Office and in other countries.

Visit us at www.eHarlequin.com

Printed in U.S.A.

CHAPTER ONE

RICO VALERON brought the long, powerful car to a smoothly purring halt outside the house and drew on the handbrake. Checking his watch briefly, he turned the key in the ignition, silencing the idling engine. He had plenty of time, he told himself, and settled back in his seat, waiting.

From her bedroom, Felicity heard the sound of the vehicle's arrival just seconds before she heard her father hurry from the dining room into the hallway.

'Your car's here!' he called up the staircase, the sound of his voice echoing slightly. 'Are you ready?'

Am I ready? she asked herself, looking into the grey eyes of her own reflection in the dressing-table mirror, then immediately away again. She didn't like what she saw in those eyes. They gave too much away.

'Fliss!' Joe Hamilton was getting impatient now. 'Did you hear me? The car's here—we should be going.'

'Just a moment!'

Felicity had trouble forcing her voice to work, making it strong enough to carry from her bedroom to the ground floor. In spite of all her efforts it didn't sound right. It had no strength, no conviction. It didn't sound at all believable.

Not at all the way a bride should sound in the moments just before she set out on her way to her wedding.

But then this wasn't the sort of wedding she had ever planned. Not the one she had dreamed of as a young girl. The wedding she had created in her fantasies, lying awake in her bed in the throes of her first adolescent crush. Then, she had imagined herself as Cinderella or Queen Guinevere, with her groom as a mixture of Prince Charming and one of the knights of the round table coming towards her astride a white charger, ready to sweep her off her feet and carry her off into the perfect 'happily ever after'.

Not like this.

Not like this travesty of a marriage that she had been forced into by fear and desperation and had tried every possible way she could imagine to get out of. But without success.

'Felicity!'

Her father was getting impatient now. He only ever used the full version of her name when he was annoyed with her and she could sense the exasperation behind the word, could picture him pushing back his shirt cuff to glance at his watch in irritation.

'I'm coming!'

What else could she say? She had no alternative. There was no knight on a white horse galloping to her rescue. She hadn't even been able to confide in her own mother. That would have meant revealing just what an appalling mess her father had made of things, the hole he had dug himself into, so deep that there was no hope of ever finding his way out.

Unless she went through with this.

'Just a minute!'

Drawing in a deep, sighing breath, she turned to the mirror once more, checking her appearance.

The white silk dress Edward had insisted on fitted her perfectly, its softly flowing lines enhancing her slender height, the sleeveless, off the shoulder style revealing slim arms and smooth skin touched by the golden tint of the sun. Her pale blonde hair was pulled away from her face, and coiled at the back of her head, under the fall of the veil that cascaded down from the delicate tracery of a small tiara. The severe style emphasised the fine bones of her face, the high, slanting cheekbones and the wide, soft grey eyes.

But there was no colour in her skin under the carefully applied cosmetics; no light in the shadowed depths of her eyes.

Instead she looked like someone about to set out on the walk to the scaffold.

'No one's going to believe this for a second,' she told her reflection fiercely. 'Can't you at least manage a smile?'

But no—that was much, much worse. The smile she switched on was so blatantly false it was almost a grimace and hastily she let it slide again, lifting her long skirts and heading for the door.

'At last!' Joe exclaimed as he saw her descending the stairs towards him. 'We're going to be late!'

'Isn't that a bride's prerogative?' Felicity returned, hiding her apprehension under a mask of insouciance. 'And Edward will wait.'

Oh, yes, Edward would wait. He stood to gain so much from this travesty of a marriage. Much, much more than he had ever promised Felicity for her agreement.

Catching the blurred signs of movement through the frosted glass of the front door, Rico abandoned his apparently indolent pose and straightened up. Narrowed dark eyes took in his surroundings in a swift, appraising survey, and he nodded in grim satisfaction.

There was no one around. Everyone had been invited to the wedding of the year and even the staff had been given the day off to stand outside the cathedral and watch the guests arrive. If his luck held he should be able to manage this totally unobserved. As the door opened he slid out of the driver's seat, one hand slipping unobtrusively into his pocket.

'We're just coming!' Joe shouted to the waiting chauffeur as he waved his daughter out of the house. 'Come on, come on, Fliss! You'll have Sir Lionel thinking... Oh, what's that now?'

Felicity turned her head in the direction of the phone which had started to ring back inside the house, suddenly a prey to a renewed rush of nerve-twisting uncertainty.

'Leave it,' she said. Now that they were on their way she wanted this over and done with.

But her father was incapable of ignoring the insistent summons.

'You go on, darling,' he said, already turning back. 'I'll just deal with this and then...'

Left alone, Felicity found herself unable to move. Her feet seemed frozen to the spot, her mind refusing to function. The intense wave of inexplicable fear was like a cold shadow chasing over her skin, making her shiver in spite of the heat of the July sun. She could see nothing, sense nothing that might have sparked it off, and yet...

'Miss Hamilton?'

It was the chauffeur who had spoken, bringing her eyes to focus on him properly for the first time. Images bombarded her already sensitive nerves, giving her a confused impression of a very tall, impressive figure, not at all what she had expected of a professional driver.

He stood straight and proud by the gleaming silver-grey Rolls, an almost military discipline about his bearing. Straight shoulders under the black uniform jacket, a strong chest tapering to a narrow waist and long, long legs. Highly polished shoes, so elegant they looked almost hand-made, were set squarely on the ground, and one black leather-gloved hand held the rear door of the car open invitingly.

But his face was hidden underneath the peaked cap and, even squinting hard against the brightness of the sun, she couldn't make out a single one of his features.

'It is Miss Felicity Hamilton?'

He sounded almost surprised, as if she was not quite

what he had expected, and the faint hint of an accent—
Spanish, perhaps?—that she had caught as he first spoke
was stronger now. Rich and husky, it turned the syllables
of her name into a murmured enticement, one that curled
seductively around her senses.

Fayleeseetay, he had said, and suddenly the shiver of
apprehension she had felt earlier was transformed into a
very different response. The tingle of pure excitement that
zigzagged down her spine was totally inappropriate in a
bride setting out to her wedding to another man. Or it
would be, Felicity told herself, if she was marrying someone she truly cared about.

'Felicity,' she corrected crisply, hiding the pang of regret
that twisted inside her behind the careful control of the
English form of her name. 'That's right.'

She must look like a dithering fool, standing here in the
middle of the drive, as if she couldn't make up her mind
where to go. And the way that the chauffeur was watching
her only aggravated that feeling of discomfort, making her
feel uncomfortably like something not too pleasant that he
had dissected and examined under a microscope.

'Felicity Jane Hamilton—soon to be Felicity Jane
Venables.'

Gathering her distracted thoughts hastily, she caught up
her skirts in a grip that was far too tight, crushing the beautiful silk impossibly, as she marched down the path towards
him.

'But you knew that, didn't you? After all, that's why
you're here.'

His silence was just a heartbeat too long, tugging at already tightly drawn nerves, stretching them out to the point
of discomfort.

'Yes, Miss Hamilton,' he said softly. 'That is exactly
why I am here.'

His eyes were dark, such a deep, ebony brown that they

were almost black, and his skin had a smooth olive tone that made her fingers itch to reach out and touch it. A straight slash of a nose combined with a squared, determined jaw to speak of a strength that bordered on ruthlessness, but the mouth told a very different story. Beautifully shaped and surprisingly soft, it made her long to see him smile, to feel the caress of those lips on her skin, to...

'Won't you get into the car, Miss Hamilton?'

'I—oh—yes...'

Distracted from the wantonly sensual path her thoughts had been drifting along, Felicity could only blink in confusion and embarrassment, a wave of hot colour flooding her cheeks. That intent, probing gaze was so powerful, so unwavering, she almost felt that he could see into her mind, read the fantasies she wanted to keep hidden from him.

The fantasies she shouldn't have been allowing herself to have! She might not love Edward, but she had promised to behave as his wife, and there was to be no hint that the marriage was anything other than a real one. That promise was going to be impossible to keep if she was already fantasising about other men and she hadn't even got the ring on her finger!

'Get into the car...'

Something had changed. Suddenly, subtly his tone had altered. A new note in it scraped uncomfortably over Felicity's unsettled nerves.

'I'm waiting for my father...'

'You can wait for him in the car.'

The note that had disturbed her was stronger now, worryingly so. In an attempt to disguise the way it had made her feel, to ignore the slow creeping of cold pins and needles over her skin, she lifted her chin and met that ebony gaze head on.

'I prefer to stay out here. I don't want to crush my dress.'

The flashing glance of those dark eyes downwards over

the dress in question was a look of pure scorn, and the shrug that lifted those broad shoulders dismissed her comment as purely feminine trivia.

'We're running late. Please get into the car, Miss Hamilton.'

It was that 'please' that did it. Something in the way it was enunciated, a dark edge that crept into his voice, moved it light years away from the common courtesy and turned it into a sound that sent something cold and unpleasant slithering down her spine.

But from inside the hall she could hear her father struggling to end the call.

'I really have to go—can we talk about this later...?'

He would be with her any moment and that knowledge restored something of the confidence that the chauffeur's disturbing attitude had chipped away at. She would get into the car, but because *she* wanted to, not because of his insistence.

She hadn't realised just how difficult it would be. Hadn't anticipated the problems of getting onto the high, soft leather seat while managing her long skirts, the enveloping veil, the silk train. She had one foot in the car when the struggle to avoid crumpling the dress resulted in an awkward loss of balance that drove a cry of shock from her lips.

'Oh!'

He was there at her side in a second. One gloved hand came out, caught the fingers that waved in panic, searching for assistance. Caught and held them, the powerful muscles in his hand and arm tensing iron-hard to support her full weight.

Within a moment she was upright again, sliding safely into the car, her dress unharmed, her position secure, and nothing but another wave of colour to give any indication of the near disaster that had just been avoided.

'Th-thank you,' she managed, shockingly aware of the fact that it was his closeness, the feel of that strength under her clutching fingertips that had put the breathless, uneven note into her voice and not any thought of the fall she had almost had.

'*De nada.*'

Strong hands arranged the folds of her skirt so that they were well away from the door, smoothed down her veil, his touch cool and totally impersonal. With the harsh force of those searching eyes turned away from her, his gaze fixed on what he was doing, Felicity found that some of the disturbing tension was seeping from her body.

She had to have been overreacting, she told herself. Had to be jumping to conclusions that were totally unjustified. She had been letting her imagination run away with her and had ended up creating a situation where none had existed.

'Thank you,' she said again, more confidently this time and when the chauffeur lifted his head again she managed to switch on a smile, directing it straight into the deep pools of his eyes.

There was no response. Nothing but the blankest, coldest stare she had ever encountered, one that turned her blood to ice in her veins and had her sinking back against the seat in sheer horror.

Her thoughts were still reeling as if that glare had been an actual physical blow so that she barely noticed the way he moved sharply, closing the door on her with a firm, decisive thud. It was only when he moved smoothly and unhurriedly round to the front of the car that she registered that all was not as she had anticipated.

Her father was still in the house, and…

'Just a minute…'

He ignored her, swinging long legs into the car and turning the key in the ignition in almost the same moment that he slammed the door to. With the Rolls in gear, he set it in motion, steering one-handed as he pulled something from his pocket and held it up. Her stomach clenching on sudden panic, Felicity realised that what he held was a mobile phone.

'Okay,' he snapped into it, his eyes on the drive ahead of him. 'Mission accomplished. You can stop now.'

'I said, just a minute!'

She was twisting in her seat, looking back to the house, watching it recede as the car picked up speed.

'Did you hear me? We can't leave yet—my father...'

The words died on her lips as the full realisation of what he had said hit home like a blow to her heart.

Mission accomplished. You can stop now.

Leaning forward, she banged hard on the glass panel that separated her from the driver.

'What are you doing? Where are we going? You can't...'

He ignored her. Thumbing off the mobile, he dropped it back into his pocket and put his hand on the steering wheel instead. With a faint roar of the engine he changed up a gear, pressed his foot on the accelerator.

'You have to stop! My father...'

Some tiny movement of his eyes, a swift glance in the rear-view mirror, alerted her. Twisting once more in her seat, she could only watch in despair as behind her she saw her father, alerted by the sound of the engine, running to the door of the house. Coming to an abrupt halt he could only stand and stare after them, shock, disbelief and total bemusement in every line of his body.

But already they were too far away for her to read his face. She saw him raise an arm, gesticulating wildly, knew that he had opened his mouth to shout but his cries were inaudible.

And then she knew. Realised just what had happened. The phone call that had distracted her father as they had left the house had been deliberately planned. It had been organised by this man to coincide exactly with their appearance, to keep her father occupied just long enough to get her into the car...

Dad!

The word formed in her brain but she was too shocked, too stunned to be able to voice it. Instead she could only watch in despair as the car accelerated again, the distance between them increasing even more. Then with one last twist of the wheel they rounded a bend in the drive and the house and her father disappeared from sight.

She was on her own, she realised fearfully. Completely on her own with this unnerving, frightening stranger.

And it was when they turned left at the bottom of the drive, in the opposite direction to the way they should have headed for the church and her wedding that she really began to worry.

CHAPTER TWO

'JUST what do you think you're doing?'

Giving into panic was quite the wrong approach, Felicity told herself. Okay, so she had been badly thrown for a minute there, but really there was no need for that. This wasn't the nightmare it seemed. No, there was simply some mistake, that was all.

'I said... Oh, can't you just slow down a bit?'

Had he even heard her? The solid, square set of his back seemed impervious as a brick wall and, with his face turned firmly in the direction they were travelling, his eyes on the road ahead, there was no way she could even read his expression or judge if she was getting through to him.

'You're going the wrong way!'

No response. Not even a flicker of a glance in her direction, not a turn of his head. If anything, his grip seemed to tighten on the steering wheel and the car engine roared again as the speedometer needle crept up.

Scrabbling frantically, Felicity managed to inch the glass panel open just a little bit and lean forward with her face close against it, her mouth in the open space.

'I said, you're going the wrong way.'

She tried to make the words sound as clear and definite as possible. After all, she was forgetting that he wasn't English—what was he? Spanish? Perhaps he just didn't understand what she was saying. Perhaps the few sentences he had spoken had been the full extent of his English, for all that they had been spoken with such apparent ease.

'Listen to me! You're...'

Frantically she scrabbled about in her memory for the

scattered remnants of the minimal Spanish she had picked up during a holiday there a couple of years ago.

'V-vaya—el camino malo,' she managed, knowing it was far from grammatically correct but at least it expressed what she *meant*.

Unbelievably, that beautifully shaped mouth twitched, twisting into a faint smile of mockery at her stumbling attempt at translation.

'Voy el camino correcto,' he shot back at her. Then, confounding her foolish belief that he hadn't understood a word she had been saying, he added sardonically, 'I am on precisely the *right* road. It's just not the direction you expected to be travelling in today.'

And while she was still gaping in stunned disbelief he added curtly, 'But wherever we're going, if you're sensible you'll sit back and fasten your safety belt. Right now the way that you're behaving is not only dangerous, it's against the law and—'

'Against the law?'

Felicity couldn't believe what she was hearing.

'Against the law? You—you're—*abducting me*—and you're worried about breaking the law on *seat belts*? Why, you...!'

With a desperate effort she managed to push the dividing window open just a little bit more and get her hand through, banging her fingers down hard on his shoulder.

'Stop this car at once! Stop it, I say!'

When he made no response but simply focused his dark-eyed gaze on the road ahead, she resorted to the only thing she could think of to get his attention. Driven past caring for her own safety, she reached up and caught hold of a strand of jet black hair that she could see underneath the uniform cap and pulled hard.

'Madre de Dios!'

For one frantic, terrifying moment the car swerved violently but a second later he had both himself and the powerful vehicle back under control.

'Stop that!' he snarled through gritted teeth. 'Don't be so damn stupid, woman! Do you want to kill us both?'

'Where you're concerned, don't tempt me,' Felicity muttered but already she was having second—and third—thoughts about the wisdom of her actions. The wild movement of the car had thrown her to one side, bruising her arm, and the few seconds of sheer panic she had felt at just the thought of what might have happened if there had been any other traffic on the road was enough to have her hastily rethinking.

She sank back onto her seat, struggling to appear outwardly calm while inside her thoughts were whirling frantically, trying to come up with some possible explanation for what was happening.

Had the chauffeur gone completely mad? What could he possibly hope for as a result of his actions?

'Look—you...' she tried again, struggling to force her voice to sound firm and full of a confidence she was far from feeling.

Those dark eyes flicked up swiftly, meeting hers in the rear-view mirror and holding her gaze for the space of a heartbeat before returning to their concentration on the road.

'My name is Rico,' he said unexpectedly.

Rico? She'd be a fool to believe that—because he'd be all sorts of an idiot to give her his real name. And one thing she didn't believe that this Rico was, was a fool. There was too much intelligence in that face, too much natural cunning in the black coffee-coloured gaze he turned on her to merit any such description.

But Rico suited him. It was a rogue's name, an outlaw's name. She could just imagine him playing the role of a brigand or a bandit in some wild adventure film.

But this was no film; nor was it, in her opinion at least, any sort of an adventure.

'Then—Rico—I think you've got this all wrong. You've made a terrible mistake.'

'No mistake.'

The flat comment was accompanied by a brusque shake of his head.

'I know exactly what I'm doing.'

'But—I think you must have the wrong person.' It was the only explanation she could come up with.

'You're not Felicity Hamilton?'

His sarcasm scraped brutally on already raw nerves.

'Well, yes, I said I was—but you've still got it wrong. I—I'm not rich, you know, and nor is my father.' She wouldn't have been forced into marrying Edward if that had been the case.

'I'm not interested in money.'

'But then—why…?'

Her voice failed completely, drying to a painful croak as she thought of the only other possible reason there might be for this man to abduct her in this way. Nightmare thoughts filled her head so that she could almost feel the colour leaching from her cheeks, her heart clenching in panic.

'Stop this car! Stop it at once!'

She had no hope that he would obey her but still it twisted every nerve to see how determinedly he ignored her, the total lack of response he made.

'I said, *stop*!'

But even as she spoke a sudden hope flared. They were approaching a particularly tricky bend. The car would have to slow down to manoeuvre round it. If she could just get the door open… Carefully she edged forward, inching her fingers onto the handle.

'It's locked.'

The words scythed through her hopes in an instant, cutting them off completely. Once more her gaze went to the mirror, meeting that knowing look with a sense of appalled horror.

'Central locking,' he supplied helpfully.

With a gesture he indicated a button on the door at his side.

'You can't get out until I let you out.'

It was foolish she knew but just for a second she ignored him. She had to. She couldn't just give in without a fight.

But no matter how hard she tugged and twisted, the door handle remained stubbornly unmoveable and at last she had to abandon the futile struggle and sit back again.

'You might as well give up and make it easy on yourself.'

Disturbingly, his voice sounded almost gentle, and he had actually managed to inject into it a faint note of concern—one that she had no doubt at all was in no way sincere.

'We have a long journey ahead of us and you'll only cause yourself more distress if you keep this up.'

'A long journey? Where are we going?'

But her attempt to sound artless and innocent didn't slip past his defences as she had hoped. Instead it earned her another of those slanting glances, half sardonically amused, half reproachful of the fact that she might think he would believe her.

'You'll find out when we get there,' he tossed over his shoulder. 'So why don't you sit back and enjoy the ride?'

'Enjoying myself is the furthest thing from my mind!'

'Well, yes…'

He moved his broad shoulders in a shrug that revealed his total indifference to her retort.

'But you'll be a lot more comfortable—and safer—if you sit back, fasten your seatbelt and try to relax.'

He was negotiating a roundabout as he spoke and, reading the road signs, Felicity saw that they were heading for the motorway that led away from her hometown and directly to London.

'You're taking a risk, aren't you?' she said sharply. 'I can read—and I can see where we're heading.'

Another indifferent shrug was his only response. Was he really so confident that he didn't care if she guessed at the route he was taking?

'Doesn't that worry you?'

'Should it?' he drawled and, as if to emphasise how little he cared, he finally pulled off the peaked chauffeur's cap and tossed it onto the seat beside him, raking one tanned hand through the sleek darkness of the hair he had revealed. Then glancing up into the mirror again, he grinned widely and wickedly just once, straight into her watchful grey eyes.

Felicity's heart kicked wildly, banging hard against her ribs and she bit down sharply on her lower lip, trying to hold back the cry of shock that almost escaped her.

It wasn't right. It wasn't *fair*! A man like this Rico—a man who had abducted her for who knew what reasons, who had invaded her life and turned it upside down—should at least look on the outside in some way that revealed the darkness of his inner heart. But in his case it was quite the opposite.

She could only see just one small part of his face reflected in the mirror but even like that, foreshortened and distorted, he had the sort of potent good looks that hit home like a punch right in her stomach.

The smooth olive skin, dark eyes and shining jet black silk of his hair all combined with strongly carved cheekbones, impossibly lush curling eyelashes and that sweetly sensual mouth to create the most forceful blueprint of purely masculine beauty she had ever seen.

She couldn't drag her eyes away but stared, transfixed,

until Rico glanced in her direction once more and caught her stunned gaze. Ashamed at being caught watching him, she looked away sharply, staring down at her hands in pained embarrassment.

'You really should fasten that seatbelt.' This time his tone made it plain that she'd do better to obey. 'We'll be hitting the motorway traffic soon and, while you might be prepared to put your life on the line by flouting the law, I would prefer that you were sensible.'

I would prefer that you were sensible. Did that mean that whatever his plans for her were they didn't include actually harming her? She couldn't tell…but rather than risk any further argument she reached for the seatbelt as instructed and pushed it firmly into the holder, relieved to find that her hands were as steady as she could have wished, betraying nothing of her inner turmoil.

'Rico what?' she asked as he turned the car onto the feed road to the motorway, the powerful vehicle increasing speed effortlessly at the slightest touch on the accelerator. 'I take it you do have a surname?'

'Just Rico will do.' His attention was on the road as he indicated, steered skilfully out into the traffic.

'I can find out, you know. Edward will tell me.'

A sign on the side of the road flashed past as she spoke, barely giving her time to register what was written on it. But, as realisation dawned, sudden inspiration struck, giving her an idea.

'In fact, I'm surprised you ever thought you'd get away with this,' she went on, talking to fill the silence, to distract him while she thought back over the scheme that had just occurred to her, considering her options, trying to decide if it would work. 'You must know I'd report you. That I'd tell Mr Venables.'

She didn't even know if he'd heard her. Not by so much as a blink of an eyelid did he betray any reaction but remained as silent and stony faced as a statue carved from marble.

'Even if this is just some sort of practical joke, he won't stand for this behaviour in one of his employees. You'll lose your job.'

Something gave him away that time. Some small, sideways slanting look, a flicker of those unbelievable eyelashes. Suddenly the truth dawned on her with an appalling sinking feeling deep in her stomach as if she had just swallowed a heavy, leaden weight.

'It isn't a job, is it?' she asked hollowly. 'I mean, not *your* job. You don't work for Edward Venables, do you?'

'I'd sooner crawl down this motorway on my hands and knees,' Rico declared and the brutal vehemence of his tone left her in no doubt that he meant what he said. A cold shiver slithered down her spine at the realisation that what lay behind that forceful declaration was a powerful antipathy that she would have to describe as nothing less than hatred.

'So this is about Edward, not me?'

And not, it seemed, about her father. Which was a relief because, after all the trouble Joe Hamilton had got himself into lately, at least he hadn't got himself entangled with this brigand of a man.

'Does that mean you're not going to…?'

She couldn't complete the sentence as another realisation rushed into her head, erasing her earlier train of thought.

'I have no intention of hurting you, if that's what you mean,' Rico put in, misunderstanding the reasons for her silence.

No, but he could ruin her life just as easily without even touching her, Felicity reflected unhappily. If she didn't turn up at the cathedral or at the very least let Edward know that it wasn't through her own choice that she wasn't there, he would wreak his vengeance on her father. Joe's crimes would be exposed, and she would have put herself through all this for nothing.

And the effect on her mother was one she couldn't even bear to think about.

The appearance of another roadside sign announcing the approach of the motorway services reminded her of her plan of a few moments earlier. It was now or never.

'I'm thirsty!' she announced and the way that her voice cracked on the words gave a conviction to her words. 'It's so hot—I really could do with a drink.'

'If you look in front of you, there's a cupboard—it's a small bar, actually. There are some plastic bottles of mineral water in there.'

'Oh, but—'

This wasn't at all what she'd had in mind. What she'd wanted was…

'You didn't really think I was going to pull in to the services and let you out, did you?' Infuriatingly, Rico seemed to have been able to read her mind. 'It's the water or nothing, sweetheart.'

'I'm not your sweetheart!' Felicity growled ungraciously, furious at having been caught out so easily. 'And I have no intention of drinking anything you've provided.'

'Then you'll have to stay thirsty,' Rico returned with cool callousness. 'I told you I had no intention of harming you.'

'And I'm supposed to believe that?'

Perversely, her pretence of being thirsty had now become a fact. The sun was beating down on the car and she was uncomfortably aware of the way that for most of the morning her tightly knotted nerves had prevented her from eating or drinking anything but the barest minimum. Just the thought of the cooled water was a temptation she found hard to resist.

'You could have laced it with anything!'

His sigh was a masterpiece of resigned patience, threaded through with exasperation.

'I give you my word—'

'The word of a kidnapper? A brute—a thug?'

In the mirror she saw him roll his eyes, just for a second.

'How about if I drank some of it myself?'

It was tempting. She really was very thirsty.

He must have seen the doubt in her face, how close she was to weakening, because suddenly he flicked the indicator and moved onto the hard shoulder, slowing the car briefly.

'Give me the water.'

She could use the bottle as a weapon, Felicity told herself as she opened the bar. She could hit this Rico on the head with it—or shake it hard until the sparkling water was fizzing so wildly that it would explode in his face as soon as he opened it.

But even as the thoughts crossed her mind, she reconsidered them hastily. If she disabled Rico, however briefly, he was still that side of the glass partition and she on the other. The control for the central locking was on his side, and she very much doubted that, even if she opened it to its fullest, she could squeeze through the gap into the front of the car.

And she didn't dare risk the possible repercussions if she angered him without incapacitating him. He might have given his word not to harm her, but that didn't mean she was prepared to risk pushing him too far.

'The water, Felicity.'

Rico had swivelled round in his seat so that he was facing her and a dark strand of warning threaded through his tone.

'Did I say you could use my Christian name?' Felicity demanded, knowing she was only being petty, using the complaint as something to hide behind, to disguise the frustration she felt at not being able to get at him in any other way.

'*Señorita* Hamilton,' Rico amended with an elaborate courtesy that only aggravated her already bad mood.

'Oh, here, take your damn water!'

She thrust the bottle at him ungraciously, trying to avoid the mockery in his dark eyes as she did so.

But not looking into his eyes meant she had to look somewhere and she was horrified by the way that, in spite of her struggle against it, her downbent gaze would keep sliding to the long, tanned line of his throat above the immaculate white collar of his shirt. The movement of his muscles as he tipped back his head, swallowing deeply, held her transfixed and she couldn't force herself to look away no matter how she tried.

A heat that had nothing to do with the sun outside dried her mouth and throat until they felt like parched sand, her whole body in the grip of a fire that would take so much more than some sips of water to extinguish.

Stop it! she told herself furiously, forcing her eyes shut and screwing them tight. She had to stop thinking this way.

'Here.'

Rico held the bottle out to her again and she almost snatched it from him. But the realisation of the way that he was observing her, made her pause again and wipe the top of the bottle with over-elaborate care that brought a scowl to his dark face.

Without thinking she gulped down all that was left in the bottle, grateful for the way that it eased the painful dryness that was tormenting her. And as she drank Rico put the car back into gear and rejoined the motorway smoothly, glancing back at her briefly as she sighed her relief.

'Better?'

'Much better, thank you.'

It was amazing how much difference just a drink could make. She felt completely refreshed, much more relaxed. The few moments' pause had given her time to collect herself, gather her thoughts. In fact if she could just work out where they were heading, maybe she could outsmart this man yet.

Buoyed up by the feeling of exhilaration, she lounged back in her seat, concentrating on looking relaxed in the hope of distracting him, making him think she had switched off. Certainly, the terrible feeling of gripping panic seemed to have ebbed just a bit.

'You're not very good at this, are you?' she asked airily. 'I guess you've never done it before.'

'And you, I take it, are an expert,' Rico returned dryly, indicating again and moving out into the overtaking lane.

'Oh, you don't have to be an expert to know you've made a couple of basic mistakes. For one...'

She held up her left hand, checking the points off on her fingers as she made them.

'You've let me find out too much—your name, for example. If in fact that is your real name.'

'Perhaps I wanted you to know exactly who I am.'

That was something that hadn't even crossed Felicity's mind but now that it had, she was forced to consider it, to wonder just why he might want her to know who he was. It didn't seem at all logical.

'And you've let me see your face,' she ticked off another point, trying not to let him see how much he had confused her.

'What did you expect? That I would wear a mask and sweep you off your feet and carry you away over my shoulder? I would think that your so efficient British police might just have noticed if that had happened.'

That, Felicity had to concede, was distinctly possible. What she was having trouble with was the disturbing im-

ages flooding into her mind at the thought of being swept
off her feet and into Rico's arms. A swift, shivering glance
at the strong, tanned fingers steering the powerful car with
skilful ease made her shudder in uncontrollable response.
Her body seemed to be growing soft and unexpectedly pli-
ant, lolling against the soft leather almost as if she was
melting in the wanton heat of her thoughts.

'So what else have you decided I've done wrong?' Rico
asked. 'What other mistakes have I made?'

Apart from the most obvious one of finding the woman
he had kidnapped—a woman who was promised to someone else—shockingly attractive? he asked himself. If he had
known that *she* was the Felicity Hamilton he had to hold
hostage, wouldn't he have had severe second thoughts
about this whole thing?

'When I think of more, I'll let you know.'

She had no intention of telling him the latest, major mistake he had made. That of letting her sit up, wide awake
and clear-eyed, in the back of the car, watching every road
sign that appeared, noting every indication of the route they
were taking. They must stop sometime and then, some way,
no matter how, she would find a way of getting in touch
with her family and letting them know just where she was.

On their right a car sped past, a young woman in the
back seat glancing into the Rolls as they did so, and something about the obvious double-take she made, the expression on her face, made Felicity giggle uncontrollably.

'What is it now?'

'I've just realised what people are seeing...'

The idea seemed crazily amusing, verging on the hilar-
ious and she hastily put up her hands to hold back another
fit of the giggles.

'I mean—what must it look like?'

She shook her head in bemusement, still grinning like a
Cheshire Cat.

'There's you—driving off down the motorway—not a church or a chapel anywhere in sight—and me—*me*—here in the back, all done up in my bridal finery…'

Something about his stillness, the swift glance of those dark eyes up to the mirror to study her closely, made her heart clench on a sudden wave of panic.

What was wrong with her? This man had kidnapped her—abducted her! There was nothing to laugh at, nothing even remotely amusing, about her situation. She should be scared. She *was* nervous—and yet…

Another attack of the giggles threatened.

'Thass another mishtake you've made. Which is one, two…'

Her eyes seemed to have blurred and the finger she tried to count with kept missing the other hand completely.

'I mean…fancy kidnapping a *bride*!'

The laughter stopped suddenly, changing to a wide, jaw-cracking yawn. Her eyelids felt heavy and, try as she might, she really couldn't focus at all. The world was sliding out of balance in the most peculiar way.

'Lie down, Felicity!' It was a sharp command from the man in the front of the car. 'Lie down at once—believe me, you'll feel much better like that.'

'Lie…'

Her eyes slid closed; her head drooped like a wilting flower, then abruptly jerked up again. Wide, dazed eyes, their pupils heavy and vastly dark, were turned on him in bitter reproach.

'What have you done to me?'

'Go with it, *gatita*. Don't try to fight it. It will be easier for you that way.'

Don't fight it!

Her heart was fluttering frantically like a small, trapped bird beating its wings against a cage. She tried to force her

eyes open, managed it just a little but her lids were too
heavy.

'Sleep, little one.'

The low, husky voice was all that she could concentrate
on. Blending in with the purr of the car's engine, it wove
a soft smoky spell around her senses.

'Duerme…'

But she *couldn't* sleep. She had to stay awake. She had
to…

The effort was too much. With a faint sigh she stopped
struggling, slumped back against the seat and slept.

Watching her, Rico clenched his big hands tight over the
steering wheel until the knuckles showed white and cursed
savagely in his native language.

If there had been any other way… But he had been
forced into this—she had forced him into this. She and that
fiancé of hers, Edward Venables.

The dark eyes blazed with fury, every muscle clenched
taut and he slammed his fist hard against the wheel. Damn
Edward Venables! Damn him to hell. Rico already owed
that louse for the way he'd treated Maria—and now he
owed him for this too. Big time.

CHAPTER THREE

'Miss Hamilton...Felicity...'

She'd heard that voice before, in her dreams, Felicity thought as she stirred reluctantly. It was the sort of voice that belonged in a dream, low and soft and sexily accented, with a way of turning her name from a simple four-syllable word into a string of poetry just by saying it.

In her dream it had belonged to a fantasy man, too. The sort of man she had never encountered in real life and never would now. Because now she had to wake up. Now she had to face reality, and reality was that today she was obliged to marry Edward Venables. It was either that or see her father go to prison for a long time.

But perhaps she could manage a few moments more in the dream world, she thought, trying to snuggle back down in the bed.

'Felicity...*gatita*...wake up.'

She looked like the kitten he had called her, lying there, curled up, soft and sleepy, her head pillowed on her hands, Rico thought unwillingly. She looked delicate and vulnerable in a way that stabbed a knife into his conscience and twisted it hard.

And he couldn't afford a conscience. Not where she was concerned. Maria's future, and that of her unborn child, depended on him being strong and dealing with this as he had promised.

'You can do this for me, can't you, Rico?'

His half-sister's voice sounded in the back of his head so clearly that he could almost see her tearstained face before his eyes, feel her hands clutching at his as she pleaded with him.

'You can see Eddie, tell him he can't go through with this wedding. That he can't marry this woman, this Felicity Hamilton...'

She had made it sound so easy, so straightforward. Because to Maria it was straightforward. She wanted this and what she wanted she usually got. But, this time, what Maria wanted had proved unexpectedly difficult to obtain.

Which was why he was here, now, with a half-conscious woman on his hands and a situation that was rapidly running right out of control.

'Felicity...'

In the back of the car, Felicity Hamilton stirred slightly, frowning faintly, and muttered something in her sleep. The white, soft veil had fallen forward over her face and instinctively he reached forward to move it aside. Then immediately wished he hadn't.

He doubted if he would ever forget the sense of shock that had hit him straight in the chest when she had appeared outside the house just a few short hours earlier. Whatever else he had been expecting of the Felicity Hamilton described to him by both Maria and the private investigator he had put on the case, it had certainly not been this.

Not this slender, delicate creature whose gentle beauty had knocked him so far off balance that his thought processes had become scrambled. In the end he had only been able to function by forcing himself to concentrate on the plan he had worked out and nothing else.

The picture Maria had painted had been of someone far tougher; someone who knew exactly what she wanted in life and went for it, ignoring anyone who got in the way. Like father, like daughter, she had said. And the detective had been equally damning.

'She goes straight from work to that nightclub, every night, Mr Valeron. Never home before near dawn.'

But this woman didn't look anything like the picture he had built up in his mind. Of course, that picture might still be the truth internally; it was just the external appearance that was different. But if that was the case then she had no damn right to be so deceptively lovely—it complicated matters far too much.

'Señorita…Felicity…'

The voice was back in her dreams, but as she stirred again Felicity found that her bed was nothing like as comfortable as usual. It felt hard and narrow and she was curled up uncomfortably. She was tangled up in something too, something that rustled and confined her, like yards of netting and…

Shock jolted her awake, making her heart slam hard against her ribcage.

This wasn't a dream. She had fallen asleep and forgotten where she was, but now the reality came rushing back.

'You!'

Her eyes flew open, wide and dark, the last remnants of the clinging sleep that had enveloped her clearing rapidly as she stared uncertainly up into his face.

'What did you do to me?'

Crazily, foolishly she actually felt betrayed. He had promised not to harm her and even as the words had left his lying mouth he had been breaking that promise. But what should she have expected from a man who was prepared to commit the crime of kidnapping in order to get his revenge on someone?

'You drugged me!'

'The mildest of sedatives only.'

The handsome face revealed no sign of guilt or repentance and the dark chocolate eyes regarded her with cool indifference.

But what had she expected? Pity or concern? She would be all sorts of a blind, deluded fool even to hope for such a thing from this cold-hearted brute.

'I thought it might help you relax. I had never anticipated that it would have the effect on you that it did.'

No, Felicity thought ruefully. There was no way he could have known that weeks of stress had meant that she hadn't had a decent night's sleep for an age. Even the weakest sedative would have knocked her for six, she was so tired.

'I didn't expect to end up with Sleeping Beauty on my hands.'

He was actually smiling—almost making a joke out of this! If she hadn't known better, she might actually have thought that he was flirting with her. But she had learned her lesson fast. She would never trust the cold-hearted monster ever again. Even if those deep brown eyes did warm with an unexpectedly soft light, and the beautifully carved mouth looked so kissable when it curved into...

What *was* she thinking of? Hastily closing off the dangerous route her wayward thoughts had opened up, she switched on a ferocious glare instead.

'I'm sure you had every move planned with a military precision. But you won't get away with it, you know!'

'No?'

One jet-black eyebrow quirked upwards, cynically questioning her furious assertion.

'You think not?'

'I *know* not!'

Felicity struggled up into a half-sitting position, feeling dangerously vulnerable lying down with him looming over her, his face in part shadow where he had blotted out the sun.

'For one thing, there are laws against such behaviour. And, for another, by now my father will surely have informed the police. You didn't exactly hide the number of your car and...'

Something about his face, some tiny flicker of response in the depths of those stunning eyes alerted her.

'What is it?' she demanded. 'What have you done?'

But even as the urgent question left her lips the haze of fear and confusion that had clouded her thoughts in the moments of wakening was slowly receding. Her eyes were starting to focus properly, her mind to take in more detailed impressions of her surroundings.

She was still in a car, it was true, still on the back seat of some large, luxurious vehicle. But, now that she looked more closely, she became aware of some very distinct differences between this car and the Rolls Royce in which she had originally fallen asleep.

Where the soft leather of the seat had once been a light fawn, now it was uncompromisingly black. There was no dividing glass panel between her and the seat where the driver—where Rico would have sat. And as she levered herself fully upright at last she saw not the silvery grey metalwork of the original Rolls but the sleek black lines of a very different car altogether.

'This isn't your car!'

'Correction,' Rico returned imperturbably. 'This is very definitely my car—my personal property. The Rolls was not. It was the one that Venables hired for you, but it was easy enough to acquire it for my own use. Your original driver was only too pleased to be given the day off, especially when he earned a fat bonus at the same time.'

I just bet he was, Felicity thought, struggling against a swamping wave of misery. The memory of her own foolishness in telling him that his kidnapping hadn't been the most efficient possible came back to haunt her in horrifying detail. How could she have been so reckless—so crazily stupid? She had even *laughed* at him, for heaven's sake!

'You...'

The black tide of horror made her voice shake and she shrank back against the far door of the car, getting as far away from him as was possible.

'How—how did you get me from the Rolls into this...?'

The faint smile grew, curving into a wicked, malign grin.

'Isn't that obvious, *gatita*? I carried you.'

Her throat closed up at the thought, her stomach heaving nauseously. The image that her mind threw up of herself in his arms, her body limp and totally at his mercy, her eyes closed, all defences down, made her shudder in appalled distress.

'How dare you?'

To her relief anger came to her aid, the hot, thick force of it driving her fear before it.

'How dare you even *touch* me!' Her voice rose high and tight and her grey eyes flashed fire in defiance. 'You had no right! No right at all! If you ever do that again, I'll kill you!'

To her fury, her reaction only seemed to amuse him, his smile incensing her further.

'So the kitten has claws,' he murmured with silky mockery. 'I can see I shall have to be prepared to defend myself.'

If her rage had been merely an annoying fly, easily flicked away and dismissed, he couldn't have made his contempt more obvious. The disdain with which he shrugged off her impotent threat had her clenching her hands tight against her thighs, struggling with the impulse to use them on that arrogantly handsome face.

'Oh, go to hell!' she spat furiously. 'Just leave me alone!'

'Willingly,' he responded smoothly. 'But I can't help thinking that you would be much more comfortable inside. You can't stay in this car all night. For one thing, I think the weather is about to change.'

A quick glance at the sky confirmed the truth of his words. The brilliant sun of earlier in the day had been eclipsed by gathering clouds, which were growing thicker and darker by the minute. But it was worse than that. Some of the intensity of the sun had also faded, leaving her in no doubt that the evening was drawing in. Just how long had she been unconscious while they were on the road? How far could they possibly have travelled in that time—and to where?

'And I'm sure you must be getting hungry. If you just come into the house—'

'No.'

Felicity shook her head firmly, her chin setting stubbornly. 'I'm not going anywhere with you. You can't make me.'

His sigh was a blend of exasperation and resignation.

'Felicity, *querida*, you cannot stay out here.'

'I can do whatever I want! And it's Miss Hamilton to you!'

Damn him, he was laughing at her again, the soft sound of his amusement adding fuel to the fire of indignation blazing inside her.

'Don't be foolish, *gatita*. You must be stiff and uncomfortable, and in need of something to eat and drink. Come with me...'

The appalling thing was that she was tempted. That the strong, tanned hand he held out to her actually looked as if it was proffered in a gesture of friendship, of assistance. But she'd been caught that way once before and she didn't intend to let it happen all over again.

'*Señorita.*' The edge to his voice revealed how much she was testing his patience. 'You are not making this easy on either of us. If you would just come inside then we could handle this situation in a much more civilised manner.'

'I don't want to make anything *easy* for you! And, quite frankly, "civilised" in the last word I could ever use to describe you! Nothing on earth could ever induce me to set foot inside that house—'

'Not even if I promise to let you phone your family?' Rico inserted smoothly, interrupting the flow of her tirade.

'Phone?'

Abruptly all the fight left her with the speed of the air

being expelled from a punctured balloon, leaving her limp and weak.

'You'd let me do that?'

The arrogant dark head moved in a swift nod of acquiescence.

'But only if you come inside.'

His tone was huskily seductive, pure enticement in a silky murmur. It was the voice that the serpent must have used to tempt Eve in the Garden of Eden and Felicity found herself weakening dangerously.

The longing to speak to her parents, to hear a friendly voice in the middle of this nightmare was overwhelming. She had never felt so alone, so lost and anxious—not even on the day that she had discovered precisely how much of a mess her father had made of his life, the dangers he had created for his family.

'The first thing you can do as soon as you are inside is ring your parents, reassure them that you are well. I'm sure they would be glad to hear from you.'

They would be going out of their minds with worry. Hot tears rushed into Felicity's eyes at just the thought.

'You wouldn't deceive me about this?'

The sheen of moisture in those dove-grey eyes was Rico's undoing. If there was one thing he had never been able to cope with, it was a woman in tears. Maria had wept all over him when she had found out about Edward Venables' forthcoming marriage and that was why he was here, now, seeing this woman's tears threaten and knowing that he was the cause of it.

'Trust me on this,' he said huskily.

Once more that big, strong hand was held out to her, and this time, after a moment's hesitation, she tentatively put her own into it. The way that her fingers disappeared when he folded his around them was almost shocking; the paler skin swallowed up by the tanned power of his grasp.

'Come, *belleza*,' he encouraged. 'Come with me.'

And slowly, cautiously, she let herself be drawn with him, sliding over the soft leather of the seat. She was almost out of the car when a new idea came to her, flashing into her mind with a force like lightning so that for a second she paused, one foot just reaching out to the ground, wondering if she could possibly risk it.

She had no idea at all where she was. The car was parked at the top of some wide, winding drive, thickly lined with trees. Just a few yards away stood a large, elegant house, the heavy wooden door already open onto a wide, spacious hall. Clearly, Rico had unlocked the door before he had come back to the car to waken her.

The house or the drive? Felicity asked herself, mentally veering backwards and forwards between the two options.

The drive must lead to a road—but how far away—and what was beyond that? And if she ran for the drive, then Rico could simply get into the car and come after her. Hampered as she was by the long skirts of her dress, the delicate satin shoes with their fine, high heels, she doubted if she could manage to run very far or very fast for very long.

But if she could make it to the house then she could slam the door to and hopefully bolt it against him. He had already said that there was a phone in the hall. Even if she only managed to win herself a few free seconds, then surely it would be long enough to ring the police and scream for help? The house was her best bet.

But first she had to disable Rico, at least for a moment or two.

'Felicity?'

Her hesitation had caught his attention, which gave her the cue she wanted.

'I—I'm sorry…' she managed to sound convincingly hesitant. 'I don't feel…'

The pretence of faintness, of still feeling the after-effects of the sedative, gave her an excuse to free her hands from his, pressing them to her forehead, hiding her eyes.

'Are you not well?'

He actually sounded concerned so that she allowed herself a small, secret grin of triumph behind her concealing fingers.

'Just a little unsteady. If I could just...'

She needed to keep her hands free so, instead of taking his again, she let them rest lightly on his arm, using his strength to support her as she got to her feet.

It was a mistake that almost distracted her from her purpose. In the moment that her fingers closed over the taut, powerful muscle, the hard bone underneath the fine material of his jacket she felt her heart jolt, her breath catching sharply in her throat. An electrical sense of awareness sizzled along every nerve, making her head spin, but this time for real. Rico was so close that the unique scent of him filled her nostrils, warm, potent, musky, totally alien and yet strangely, disturbingly familiar in a way that set her pulse racing hotly.

This time her unsteadiness wasn't totally feigned as she slid out of the car and slowly stood upright, using his strength as her support. She didn't dare to look up at him, fearful that those dark, probing eyes might be able to read her feelings in her face and recognise her response for the lightning bolt of white-hot sexual awareness that it was.

'Lean on me, if you like.'

Lean on him? Felicity thought on a wave of near hysteria. If only he knew just how she longed to do just that! How her hot, throbbing, dangerously aroused body yearned to throw itself towards him, to rest against the hard wall of his chest, feel those powerful arms come round her.

No! She couldn't afford even to let herself *think* of such things or she would waver in her purpose, forget what she had planned. She had to act *now* or it would be too late.

'I...' she began, her voice convincingly low and weak.

'*Si?*'

As she had hoped, he bent his dark head towards her, in order to hear better. It was now or never.

White teeth digging into her lower lip in concentrated determination, she brought her right arm up and out, elbow bent sharply, aimed straight at that square, determined jaw. In the same moment that it connected with the hard strength of bone, jerking his head back, she launched a wild kick at his nearest ankle, allowing herself a faint smile of pleasure as she heard his muffled grunt of pain. For just a split second she was free and she took full advantage of the moment, hitching up her white silk skirts and sprinting for the door.

She only managed to get a few feet before a hard hand closed over her shoulder, pulling her back. An arm snaked round her waist, clamping tight around her slender frame, and, kicking and struggling, she was lifted bodily from the ground.

'Oh, no you don't, *señorita*!'

Rico had been anticipating the escape attempt. It was quite shocking to realise just how well he had come to know her, even on such a short acquaintance. But just the brief exchanges—he could hardly call them conversations—as they had had on the journey here, had taught him so much about the way her mind worked. He hadn't expected that she would have so much spirit. That she would be prepared to take him on quite as openly as she had. But he'd observed and learned and as a result he had had a good idea of what was coming.

It was that tiny grin that had given her away. A smile that she had thought he couldn't see but which had put a light into her eyes that warned him she was up to something. So he had been ready for the moment she attacked, anticipating the movement of her arm, ready to dodge the full force of it. The vicious little kick to his ankle was more of a surprise, but he soon recovered from that.

'You don't get away from me that easily!'

'Let me go!'

She tried to fight; tried to kick out at him again but the long skirts of her dress hampered her and the whirling veil covered her face, half-blinding her.

'Careful, *belleza*…' It came out unevenly as he fought to adjust his grip on her, trying to hold her more securely. 'You'll have us both on the ground.'

'Do you think I care?'

Furiously she writhed against his restraining hands until the only thing he could do was lift her higher, his arm going round her waist, the other supporting her legs, her head against his shoulder.

'Now perhaps you'll do as you're told!' he flung at her, clamping down hard on the sudden blaze of anger that had flared inside him, making him want to shake her roughly, drive some sense into her.

But even as he spoke Felicity moved, her arms coming out in an automatic, instinctive movement to close around his neck in order to make herself more secure. Her action brought a faint rush of perfume to tantalise his senses.

The fragrance of rose and lily was fresh and sweet, but it was what came with it that delivered the real kick, awakening everything that was truly male and sexual within him. The clean, delicate, and yet potently erotic scent of this woman's skin and hair, the feel of her warm, soft curves in his arms made his body tighten in hunger and respond with fierce arousal all between one blink and another.

And as Felicity's head went back against his shoulder and eyes the colour of an autumn mist met his own sensually darkened gaze, Rico knew that he had just made one of the worst mistakes of his life.

CHAPTER FOUR

IT HAD been bad enough when he had managed the change of cars a couple of hours earlier.

Then at least she had been deeply asleep, totally oblivious to what was going on. Her body had been limp and unresponsive, those soft grey eyes closed and hidden from him.

Now they were staring straight into his, the sparks of fury and rebellion still burning deep in them, making them shimmer in angry defiance. Her skin was flushed with the after-effects of their undignified tussle, her mouth slightly open as she tried to control her uneven breathing.

He didn't want to think that it might not just be the physical exertion that had set her pulse racing. Didn't even want to consider the possibility that she too might feel the sudden singing tension that had gripped him. Could she sense the abrupt, dangerous change in the mood of the moment, the shift in the sensual temperature that had turned it from winter chill to midsummer heatwave in the space of a heartbeat?

'I'm going to take you inside,' he growled, shocking himself with the way that his voice didn't sound like his own but had suddenly become rough around the edges, thickening revealingly. 'And if you're wise you'll not try any more crazy stunts.'

'What did you think? That I was just going to sit there and let you do what you wanted with me?'

'I'd given you my word.'

'Oh, yes, and I know just how much that word is worth.

You gave me *your word* that you wouldn't harm me even while you were feeding me drugs to knock me out.'

'I've already told you, I never planned for quite that effect.'

He was striding towards the door as he spoke; the ease with which he carried her weight a testimony to the true strength of the muscles beneath that superbly tailored jacket. And the terrible thing was that she had suddenly lost all the will to fight.

It was as if in that frantic dash towards the house she had drained what little strength she possessed, leaving herself limp and incapable of movement.

Oh, who was she trying to kid? Felicity reproached herself inwardly. Her sudden mental paralysis had nothing at all to do with her mind and everything to do with an injection of white-hot physical excitement that had set her body throbbing in urgent response. The sensations searing through her in reaction to the forceful, warm strength of Rico's taut male body so close to hers, the scent of his skin in her nostrils, the iron-hard support of the arms that held her made her skin burn until she felt she was in the grip of some delirious fever...

'And did you not think that maybe a mild sedative was perhaps a kinder way out than others I might have taken?'

'So what do you expect from me? Thanks? Gratitude for the fact that you didn't treat me any worse than you already have?'

'Oh, no,' Rico tossed back, caught on the raw by the sudden switch back to cold contempt.

For a second there she had seemed almost to treat him as a human being. But now the lady of the manor act was right back in place, those soft smoky eyes hardening to the grey of the sea on a winter's day. Immediately he felt his own feelings change in response as anger put a sharper edge on the volatile cocktail of responses he was already prey to.

'Gratitude would be the last thing I'd expect from you. After all, the woman who was going to marry Edward Venables...'

Something about her sudden stillness, the shocked, blank look in those misty eyes, brought him up short.

'Oh, come now, *querida*,' he derided sardonically. 'Don't tell me that you had actually forgotten. That it had somehow slipped your mind that today was to have been the happiest day of your life.'

She *had* forgotten, Felicity realised, her mind hazing over in shock. She could excuse herself by saying that the way Rico had exploded into her life with all the force of a whirling tornado had numbed her thoughts, making it impossible to think. But the truth was both deeper and less complicated than that.

Since the moment that she had first set eyes on this darkly devastating man, her mind hadn't been her own. It was as if he had taken possession of it, filled her every thought with the stunning force of his presence, wiping away any memories of who she had been, how her life had been.

'You didn't remember.' Rico's voice was thick with contempt. 'You...'

'Put me down!' Felicity inserted sharply, hating the scorn in his voice, hating the way he looked at her, dark eyes bleak and cold. 'Put me down at once! I can walk—'

'Oh, no, *querida*.' The hateful mockery grew sharper, lacing his tongue with cynical acid. 'How could I deny you the moment that every woman dreams of? The moment when all the fantasies of her childhood, the hopes of her adolescence come to fruition.'

The beautiful mouth had curled into a brutal sneer, the sexy accent heightening on each word. But the sound of his voice no longer made her toes curl, her skin tingle in delight. Instead it was like the lash of a cruel whip, flaying away a protective layer of skin so that she shivered at the feel of even the air against her flesh.

'Don't be cruel!' It was a cry of protest.

'Cruel, *gatita*? Cruel?' he taunted. 'I am not being cruel. I am simply ensuring that your day ends as you had hoped it would—with you in the arms of a very rich man indeed, being carried over the threshold of his house...'

As he spoke, he suited action to the words, mounting the steps to the front door, shouldering it open, carrying her over the threshold into the cool shadows of the hall.

After the light of the sun, Felicity fond that she was temporarily blinded, unable to see anything clearly. And what made matters worse were the weak tears that filmed her eyes; tears she was determined not to let fall. Rico's words had stabbed straight to her heart and twisted in it, but the truth was that they had hurt so much because they were so very far from reality.

She doubted that Edward would ever have thought to follow any of the traditions of a real wedding, at least as far as she was concerned. Once the formal, public ceremony and the lavish reception was over, he would probably have dropped all pretence at being the loving bridegroom, the part he had acted so unexpectedly well over the past month or so. Instead he would have reverted to the role of cold, calculating schemer, the man who had manipulated both her life and that of her father in order to get just what he wanted.

Right now she didn't know who was worse—Edward or Rico.

'For such a beautiful bride as you are, it is the least I can do.'

Once inside, with the door kicked closed behind them,

he paused, ebony eyes going towards a room on his left and just once, very briefly, glancing towards the stairs.

'So now that I have carried you over the threshold, *mi ángel*, what next, I wonder?'

Rico had bent his arrogant dark head down to murmur in her ear, the warmth of his breath stirring the tendrils of her hair, brushing softly against her cheek.

'If you were truly my bride—*mi esposa*—I know exactly what I would do...'

And his body knew it too. He knew he should set her down, put her on her feet and move well away. That was the sane, the only safe approach. But with her in his arms, with the scent of her skin all around him, the last thing on God's earth he felt like was playing it safe. And he certainly didn't feel *sane*. Instead he knew he was totally out of control—completely crazy and dangerously off balance.

His heart was pounding, his blood flowing hot in his veins. Every sense he possessed clamoured in hunger, insistently demanding appeasement, making him ache with need. And the feel of those soft arms around his neck, the yielding pressure of her feminine body against his chest and the brush of her hair against his neck were almost more than he could bear. He wanted to drop her straight to the floor in order to end the sweet torment and yet at the same time he wanted to hold on to her so as to prolong it for ever.

'But I'm not your bride!'

Felicity knew she had to break the spell that that low, husky voice had been weaving around her weakened senses. Listening to it had been like sliding slowly but irresistibly into a bath filled with warm, golden honey. She could feel it flowing around her, enfolding her, threatening to close over her head at any moment.

'I'm not your wife and I never will be! I'm just your prisoner, your captive—here under duress because you forced me into this! And whatever fantasies you might be harbouring, you can forget them right now! You lay one finger on me and I'll—I'll…'

'You'll do what, *belleza*?' Rico enquired with silky menace when, suddenly realising just how hollow her threat was when he already had more than a hand on her, when she was held securely in his arms, her voice died away rapidly. 'What was it you promised earlier? That you would kill me?'

The sound of his laughter was shocking. It was all the more terrifying because there was no trace of any real humour in it, only the sardonic dismissal of her impotently angry words.

'Do you know, *gatita*, it might just be worth it.'

'You don't mean that! You can't…'

'Can't I?'

Rico's smile turned her blood to ice. Now that she could see more clearly, she couldn't be unaware of the way that his pupils had darkened, enlarged, until his eyes were almost all black, only the tiniest line of the deep brown at the very edge of the iris as he looked down into her still, white face.

'The way I feel right now, I think I could die happy if I only had you in my bed for one night.'

'One night…'

She could barely get the words from her constricted throat, her voice just a raw, broken croak of disbelief.

'You're crazy!'

To her horror he nodded agreement.

'One night—but what a night, Felicity. A night that neither of us could ever forget, that we could only ever dream of in our wildest fantasies. A night when—'

'No!'

Summoning up all her strength to snap free of the hypnotic trance in which he had imprisoned her, Felicity twisted in his arms, struggling against the power of his hold. Clenching her hands into fists, she pummelled them against the powerful wall of his chest, aiming wildly at his shoulders, his arms, would have hit his face if he hadn't seen it coming and instinctively flung his head back defensively.

'Let me go! Put me down! Put me *down*!'

'Your wish is my command,' he returned, dark eyes burning into hers insolently.

Adjusting her position very slightly, he lowered her slowly to the ground in such a way that she slid all the way down the length of his body, hips, breasts and legs held so tight against the muscular strength of him that she couldn't be unaware of the blatant physical sign of his intense response to her. The swollen evidence of his passionate arousal burned against her even through the fine white silk of her skirts.

And when her feet were on the floor he still held her against him, one hard hand clamped in the small of her back, the other fastening over the fine bones of her chin, lifting her face towards his.

'I want to kiss you, *mi belleza*,' he told her in a voice that was harsh with barely controlled hunger. 'If the truth is known, I have wanted to kiss you from the first second I saw you; from the moment you came out of that house and walked towards my car. I wanted to hold you then, to take you in my arms like this, to touch your skin, inhale the scent of your hair...'

He suited action to the words, dropping his proud head so that his cheek rested against her hair, the pad of his thumb tracing the full softness of her mouth.

So he had felt it too. That immediate, lightning strike of response, that inexplicable yearning, the male to female reaction at its most primitive, most basic level. He had sensed it, as she had, on the air that they breathed, in the look from one set of dark eyes to a much lighter pair.

'And you want it too.'

'Oh, yes...'

Somehow it escaped her without a moment's thought. Thought would have told her that what she was doing wasn't at all wise. That it was beyond stupidity—it was foolish, crazy—*dangerous*. But thought didn't enter into what she was feeling in any way. She was incapable of thought. She was nothing but feeling, total emotion, pure sensation.

And she wanted the kiss she knew was coming. Wanted the feel of that beautiful mouth on her own. She hungered for the warm touch of skin on skin, the caress of his strong hands, the sensation of the silken strands of his hair under her fingertips.

And so she swayed towards him, her wild hands slowing, stilling for a moment then closing over the broad square shoulders and clinging tightly as his mouth came down on hers.

It was harder than she had imagined. Harder and more cruel so that for a second her mind seemed to split in two, hunger warring with panic as she struggled against the wild passion that threatened to burn her up alive.

Passion and hunger won. She was incapable of holding out against them, incapable of denying herself even more than she was incapable of denying him. His mouth took hers by storm, crushing and near brutal one moment then gentling to a stunning tenderness the next. The tantalising slide of his tongue was a delight and a torment combined, wakening all the most sensitive pleasure spots of her lips and mouth, making her open to him, surrendering herself completely.

'*Belleza...belleza...*' Rico crooned softly against her skin, his mouth trailing a path of fire over her face and down the fine lines of her throat to fasten fiercely on the creamy slope of one exposed shoulder. 'You are so lovely…so perfect.'

She *felt* perfect, Felicity thought shakily. She felt just right for this man, her body fitting exactly against his, her hips cradled against the strong bones of his pelvis, her legs coming between his as he shifted slightly to accommodate her. Her breasts seemed perfectly formed for the touch of his hands, a sigh of delight escaping her as his hard fingers cupped their soft weight, the heat of his palms burning through her dress to her skin.

Her flesh was on fire for his touch, her body aching to feel his against her. Her hands were in his hair, tangling tightly in the night-dark strands, closing over the strong bones of his skull, drawing his head down to hers so that she could deepen and prolong the kiss until her senses reeled in a delirium of pleasure.

'Oh, *mi ángel*…'

With a rough, impatient sound deep in his throat, he crushed her closer, impatient fingers seeking and finding the tiny pearl buttons at the back of her dress, easing them from their fastenings with a devastating efficiency. But even the speed of his actions was not enough for him and with a violent curse in Spanish he suddenly wrenched the slender straps from her shoulders and down over her arms with such force that she heard the fine silk rip shockingly.

But the devastation of the expensive garment went unheeded. She could only concentrate on one thing, her mind centred on the wild, hotly erotic sensations his touch was firing all over her body. Those strong, bronzed hands were now pushing deep inside the dress, over warm, smooth skin, forcing it down to reveal the high, pale globes of her breasts. She wasn't wearing any sort of a bra; the skilfully boned bodice had made it unnecessary and so there was no impediment to his searching touch.

She was being moved backwards all the time, walked slowly, one step at a time towards the wall at the foot of the stairs. With each movement of Rico's, one of his long, powerful legs came between her own for a second, setting up a throbbing ache between her thighs, aggravating it with the pressure of his hard body against hers.

'Rico!'

The sound of his name was pushed from her lips as she came hard up against the wall. He imprisoned her there with his broad strength, effectively blocking any way of escape as his long fingers curved underneath her breasts, lifting their soft weight free of the remaining confines of the white silk, his thumbs tracing burning erotic circles over their tight, hungry tips.

'*Rico!*'

It was a wild, keening cry as she flung back her head, her bright hair resting against the wooden panelling as she abandoned herself to the delight of his touch. With his proud head bent, he replaced the tormenting caress of his hands with the hot tug of his mouth, first on one side, then the other, making her writhe in a fury of sensual delight. The burning pulse between her legs grew more powerful with each provocative touch, the stinging delight of his suckling, until she was straining against him, grinding her pelvis against the hard swell of his arousal, making him groan aloud in his turn.

'You see, *querida*...'

Briefly he tore his mouth away from her throbbing breasts to look deep into her passion-glazed eyes.

'This is how it is. This is what has been between us from that first moment, from the second our eyes met. This is as inevitable as the sun rising every morning, as each breath following another. It has to be.'

'Has to be...'

The husky echoing of his fervent declaration was all she could manage. Even the few seconds' deprivation of his caresses was more than she could bear and the words merged into a moan of complaint, falling away wordlessly.

Her heart was racing, her breathing raw and uneven and the pulse pounded wildly in her veins. She inhaled the scent of his skin like some rawly potent drug, and her fingers scrabbled at the front of his shirt, struggling to tug open the buttons she could barely see through eyes so hazed with desire.

Rico's response was a harsh, thick sound, deep in his throat as his own hands moved lower, bunching up her long white skirts, lifting them higher, higher until the delicate lace tops of her stockings and the matching dainty panties were exposed to his urgent fingers. At the first touch of his hands at the burning centre of her femininity, stroking her softly through the fine satin, Felicity's eyes closed on a choking sigh of surrender. This was what she wanted. The union of all that was most strongly female in her to the deepest masculine drives of this man.

'So this is what we were both made for,' Rico muttered roughly in her ear. 'This is what must be between us. But you have to come willingly. It has to be your move—your choice.'

'My—choice?'

The words made no sense. Couldn't he see? Couldn't he *feel*?

'You have to tell me, *querida*…'

The low, husky voice had dropped an octave or more, becoming rougher, thicker, harsher and those deep-set eyes burned like molten metal, searching her face, probing deep into her soul.

'The bedroom is upstairs. Do I take you there, or do we stay here and make polite conversation?'

Yes! The word burned so fiercely in her thoughts that she was sure he must see it in her face, read it in her eyes, etched there in letters of fire. *Yes, yes, yes!* But somehow she couldn't get the sound past the twisting, constricting knot of emotions clogging up her throat.

'Do you want me, *gatita*?'

Did she want him? Ridiculous question! Impossible, preposterous, unnecessary question.

Of course she wanted him! She yearned for him, *ached* for him. Her body was one complete scream of hunger for him. But...

And then as suddenly as if a light had been switched on, illuminating the clouded darkness of her thoughts, she knew what was wrong.

'Do I want you?' she managed, a thread of weak near-laughter running through her words. 'But who are you? I don't even know your name. All I know is Rico—if in fact that is the truth.'

Looking into the darkness of his eyes she saw the swift change there, the move from frowning uncertainty to a new understanding and it was like watching the sun come from behind a cloud, lighting his face from within. The transformation took her breath away.

'The truth, *gatita*?' he laughed. '*Si*. Oh, yes, I told you the truth. My name really is Rico—short for Ricardo. Ricardo Juan Carlos Valeron at your service, *señorita*.'

It was like a slap in the face.

Ricardo Juan Carlos Valeron.

The words pounded into her senses like cruel blows, making her heart stop, her breath die in her lungs.

Ricardo Valeron.

If it hadn't been for the hard strength of his body pinning her to the wall she knew that her legs would have given way beneath her and she would have sunk to the floor in a limp, lifeless heap. As it was, her eyes had hazed over, seeing nothing but an out-of-focus blur, vague, indecipherable shapes that made no sense at all. And in her head was the fierce, whirling buzz of a thousand angry bees, drowning out all thought, all sense, all feeling.

'Take your hands off me!'

She said it blind and was thankful for the fact that she couldn't see his face. It was a small mercy not to be able to look into his eyes and see now, at last, the real truth. See him as he truly was, with the lies, the deceit, the pretence stripped away.

This man, the man who had kidnapped her, carried her away from her family and friends, from her one hope of putting right all her father's mistakes and repaying the money he had embezzled was Ricardo Valeron! This man on whose mercy she was totally dependent for her safety, her security, maybe even her life, was the one man she knew she should fear above all others. The one man who had the power to make an appalling situation even worse.

And now it seemed that he had done exactly that.

CHAPTER FIVE

IT WAS all her worst dreams come true at once.

Rico was Ricardo Valeron.

It was the only thing her battered, bruised mind could fasten onto. The only thing that made any sort of sense in a world gone suddenly mad. But the only form of sense it made was shadowed by such horror, such devastation that she could only think of it in snatched, fleeting seconds before her anguished brain flinched away again, unable to bear the pain.

Rico the brigand was gone, vanished for ever, destroyed by a few carelessly—even smugly—spoken words. And she couldn't believe how her foolish, desperately deceived heart cried out in distress at the thought.

She actually *missed* him. Rico the brigand had been a villain, a kidnapper, a liar—but she had come to accept that. She had almost let him charm her, come close to putting a sort of trust in him. But she hadn't known the real truth about his lies. She hadn't known the full extent of his deceit. Now she did and she felt as if her world had shattered into cruel, jagged shards of glass that threatened to savage her soul if she so much as thought about it.

'I said, take your hands off me.'

'Take…? Felicity—*querida*…'

Rico had never seen anyone change so fast or so completely. One moment he had been holding a hotly willing, sensually responsive woman in his arms. The next moment it was as if her blood had frozen in her veins, turning her into an immobile ice woman from head to toe. The transition took only seconds, bringing him up hard against this new reality so fast that he actually felt bruised by it, his body jarred by the force with which hers repelled him even though she hadn't moved or even touched him.

'And don't you dare ''*querida*'' me! I'm not your darling—I'm not *anything* to you! And that's exactly the way I want it.'

'What the…? *Por Dios, señorita*—what is going on here?'

'Not what you thought was going on—that's for sure!' Felicity flung at him, turning on him a glare of such loathing that he actually took half a step backwards, stiffening sharply, his hands loosening so that the freed silk skirts slithered back into place around her legs. 'And nothing else is going to happen—*nothing*! I'd rather die!'

'Is that die in the same way that you vowed to kill me if I so much as touched you again?'

Shock combined with blank confusion and the slow beginnings of the cruel ache of frustration to blacken his mood. Already his fiercely aroused senses were beginning to realise that the sexual release, the consummate fulfilment they had been expecting was now to be denied them. And the nagging complaint blended with his already off-balance state to create a cold fury that was impossible to suppress.

'Well, look at me, *darling*—look at me!'

His hands flew out in a wild, expressive gesture, drawing her attention to his obviously uninjured state.

'I touched, all right—did more than touch! I kissed you, caressed you. I all but stripped the dress from your body and you didn't even protest—not so much as a single letter of the word ''no'' passed your lips.'

'That…' Felicity began huskily, but he ignored her, swept aside her weak attempt at an interjection as the words flowed out like the rush of a flood swollen river, impossible to contain.

'I could have had you right here—against the wall and

you would have been urging me on. But now you freeze like an ice maiden or a nun who's taken a vow of chastity.'

'That was before I knew who you were!'

She flung the words in his face, desperate to have them said, as much for her own sake as out of any need to explain to him.

Ricardo Valeron. She had let Ricardo Valeron touch her, kiss her…more. Her skin crawled just to think of it.

Far, far too late, Edward's warning sounded in her ears.

'The one man you really must beware of—the one who could do your father some real damage—is Ricardo Valeron. He's a cut-throat—vicious, ruthless, and totally without morals. He won't just see the money Joe owes him as a financial debt but as a personal insult and, if he found out that your Papa has been fiddling the books, he'll want blood in reparation. He's Argentinian, you see. Latin blood and all that.'

Argentinian. Not Spanish as she had first thought. Miserably Felicity cursed herself for not realising sooner. For not even suspecting.

'Before you knew who I was?' Rico pounced on her words. 'So you know of me, then? You've heard my name?'

'Of course I've heard it! My father's your accountant. And I'm—I was—I'm supposed to be marrying Edward. I know you and he are business rivals.'

She also knew that it was common knowledge that there was no love lost between her supposed fiancé and this man. That commercially and personally they had been at daggers drawn for a year or more.

'Rivals is something of an understatement,' Rico muttered, dark threat lacing the words with danger so that Felicity shivered apprehensively.

If only she knew exactly why he had abducted her like this. Was it because of her 'fiancé's' business interests—to ensure that some valuable contract went the way Rico wanted?

Or, even more worrying, was it because of whose daughter she was? Did he want her as a hostage to ensure her father's behaviour and the repayment of the money Joe owed? Because if it was the latter—her skin crawled with horror at the thought—it would be a long, long time before she was free. That amount of money wasn't easily come by; in fact her father would find it impossible to raise. Wasn't that why she had committed herself to this travesty of a marriage to Edward? Because she could see no other way out.

'It's good to see that at least you remember your abandoned groom,' Rico added, his dark-eyed gaze searing over her, black with vicious contempt. 'Even if the concern is a trifle belated to be sincere.'

'Of course I remember him!' Hastily Felicity tried to recover the ground she knew she had lost dangerously. 'He must be going crazy with worry.'

'On the contrary, I think you'll find that he has had plenty to occupy him—so much so that I doubt if he'll even have noticed your absence.'

His smile had nothing of warmth in it but was cold and merciless like the flick of a cruel whip.

'It seems to me that the two of you would have been supremely well matched. Tell me,' he went on, lounging back against the wall and subjecting her to a slow insolent survey from the top of her head to the narrow fine-boned feet in the elegant shoes. 'That white dress. Are you actually entitled to wear it or is it, like so many others these days, purely for show and to hide a multitude of sins?'

'That's no business of yours!' Felicity snapped but unfortunately the effect of the defiance she was aiming for was ruined by the sudden evaporation of all her mental strength as an unfortunate glance down reminded her of just what a sight she looked.

The bodice of her beautiful dress still hung bunched up around her waist, pushed there by Rico's impatient hands, and her high, smooth breasts were exposed to that searing gaze, the delicate skin still bearing the reddened marks of his passion, the faint abrasions inflicted by his hands and mouth.

Fiery colour flooded her face and neck as she hastily and awkwardly grabbed at the creased garment, pushing her arms into the sleeves and shrugging it up around her shoulders again. And that was as much as she could manage. Fastening the dozens of small pearly buttons that went down her back was totally beyond her. That had been the last task her mother had performed before setting out for the cathedral and one it was impossible to do for herself. The only alternative was asking Rico for help and that was an idea that didn't even have time to actually cross her mind before she rejected it violently.

So she had to be satisfied with folding her arms in front of her in order to hold the dress up and struggling to ignore the way it gaped and sagged at her shoulders and back, threatening to slide revealingly with every move.

'You promised me a phone call,' she declared tartly, anxious to claw back some degree of self-possession from a situation that was rapidly crumbling to pieces in her hands.

'Be my guest.'

Rico reached into his pocket and pulled out the slim silver mobile phone she had seen him using in the car earlier at the start of her ordeal.

'Oh, but… But I thought…'

'You thought that I would have a regular phone here in the hallway that you could use under supervision now, but hope to sneak away to, to use again privately later to let everyone know where you are,' Rico supplied, seeing her disturbed grey gaze search the hallway for exactly that. 'Do you really take me for so much of a fool, *querida*? Do you think that because I'm "not very good at this"—' sardonically he quoted her own impetuous words in the car back at her '—that I will have no idea of exactly how your mind is working and the sort of schemes you're planning on coming up with to outwit me? Credit me with a little common sense.'

She'd have to credit him with a lot more than that, Felicity thought unwillingly. Right now she could almost believe that he possessed the ability to read her mind. Certainly, whatever she did it seemed that he was one step ahead of her at every point, recognising and thwarting her plans with an insulting lack of effort.

'Just give me the phone,' she growled ungraciously, holding out a hand as far as was possible while still ensuring she was covered up, an embarrassed exclamation escaping her as the gaping dress slipped precariously.

Rico regarded her struggles with an undisguised amusement, a fiendish gleam in the depths of his dark eyes.

'Don't you think it's a little too late to worry about preserving your modesty?' he drawled derisively, that taunting gleam deepening as he spoke. 'After all, there's nothing there I haven't already seen—and more.'

'Which doesn't mean that I'm going to offer you a peep show whenever you fancy it! From now on, you keep your prying eyes and wandering hands strictly to yourself.'

Felicity drew herself up, her chin lifting defiantly, grey eyes glacial, as she gathered the shattered remnants that were all that remained of her dignity around her.

'The phone…' she prompted coolly.

It was the Lady of the Manor act again. The one that had already set his teeth on edge several times in what was turning out to be a very long, very wearing afternoon. Felicity Hamilton was not at all what he had been led to expect, and as a result, his own behaviour had become so unpredictable that he barely even recognised himself.

What the hell had possessed him to come on to her like that, with all the finesse and subtlety of a rampant bull? He was long past the age when his hormones ruled his head and yet he had come close to being totally out of control in a way that he would have sworn was totally alien to him. Normally he prided himself on treating women with respect and consideration, but with this woman all that carefully learned finesse had evaporated like mist before the sun.

But she'd been with him every inch of the way. She'd needed no persuading, shown no sign of hesitation or doubt. In spite of the fact that she had been on her way to marry one man, she had responded to him as if he was the only male in the world for her, in a way that proved the fancy white dress to be a complete mockery of the symbol of purity it traditionally was.

Maria had been right. This woman had the morals of an alley cat and deserved to be treated as such.

'The phone...' Felicity repeated, injecting as much ice into the words as she could manage.

She knew she'd caught him on the raw when she saw the flare of something dangerous in those deep dark eyes. But he punished her for her petty triumph immediately, deliberately tossing the phone towards her so that it fell short of the reach she could manage while still holding on to her dress. After an undignified scramble she managed to catch it—just—and hastily dialled her father's mobile number before Rico could intervene.

'You do realise that this will mean your number comes up on Dad's phone?' she flung at him, the note of triumph at actually outmanoeuvring him lifting her voice.

Infuriatingly he looked totally unfazed.

'You do realise that that's exactly what I want?' he tossed back, parodying her voice with wicked accuracy.

'You want...? Oh, *Dad*!' Her voice cracked revealingly as the phone was answered and she heard Joe Hamilton's reassuring deep tones. 'Dad, it's me—it's Fliss.'

'Fliss, darling, at last!'

Something was wrong. Something about her father's tone jarred uncomfortably. It wasn't at all what she had expected. But, after the shocks and disturbances of the day her brain was too bruised, too out of focus to register exactly what it was.

'I was wondering when you would call.'

'You...'

Her thoughts reeled as she realised just what it was that was nagging at her so uncomfortably. Just what had set all her senses on red alert, screaming warning signals automatically.

Her father wasn't shocked. He didn't even sound distressed or worried. And yet he must have been waiting for her call for three or more hours now. Three hours of knowing that his daughter who he had last seen disappearing down the drive in a car driven by a complete stranger had seemed to have vanished off the face of the earth. Three hours of knowing that she hadn't turned up for the wedding that was going to save his skin and that he had no idea at all where she was.

And he didn't seem in the least bit concerned.

'Dad?'

Shock made her voice quaver uncertainly on the word. 'How's Mum?'

It was the question that was uppermost in her mind. The thought of her frail mother, already being told to take things easy, avoid any sort of stress because of her weak heart, being subjected to the anxiety of the past few hours worried her sick. What if something had happened? A stroke? Worse?

'Your mother's fine.'

Once again, Joe's easy voice was like a shock to her system.

'But then, of course, she never wanted you to marry Edward in the first place.'

No, Felicity reflected. Her mother had been the one person she hadn't been able to deceive. Claire Hamilton had seen through the careful part her daughter had been acting for the past few weeks and picked up the anxiety and panic behind it. Felicity had tried to assure her that her only problem was pre-wedding nerves but she knew she hadn't been entirely convincing.

'She just hopes you know what you're doing.'

Doing?

'Dad...' Drawing a deep breath, Felicity decided that taking a risk was the only way. 'Dad—I'm with Valeron.'

Her eyes flew to where Rico stood silently against the wall, ebony eyes alert and watching every move, every flicker of emotion across her face. Tensing fearfully, she nerved herself for what she thought would be his inevitable reaction, anticipating that he would launch himself angrily towards her, snatching away the phone in fury at what she had revealed.

Surprisingly, it didn't come. Instead he seemed quite content to simply wait and watch.

'I—Ricardo—'

'Yes, we know.'

To her consternation, once again her father failed to react to what she thought would send him into a fit of panic. Instead, amazingly, he actually laughed.

'Edward was furious at first, but now he has other things to occupy his mind.'

'*How* do you know?'

What had they received? A ransom demand? Some other sort of a threat? But if that was the case, then surely her father wouldn't appear quite so calm and relaxed.

'Dad—what's going on?'

'Going on, sweetheart? Well, I would have thought that you'd be the one to tell us that. After all, you're the one who's snared Valeron.'

'Snared...'

Felicity actually took the phone away from her ear and stared at it in total disbelief. Her father couldn't have said what she thought she'd heard. It was impossible! But he had sounded so ridiculously good-humoured. A new, worrying suspicion slid into her mind.

'Dad—are you drunk? Look—can I speak to Edward?'

But it was as if the sound of the other man's name was like a goad to Rico, pushing him into sudden action.

'That's enough,' he snapped, taking two swift strides forward, his hand coming out to take the phone from her.

Pausing only long enough to speak the four crisp words, 'I'll be in touch,' into the mouthpiece, he switched it off, clicking the cover shut and pushing it deep into the inner pocket of his jacket.

'I was using that!' Felicity protested, her hand going out to retrieve the phone, only to find herself blocked as Rico's hard bronzed fingers clamped firmly around her wrist holding her still. 'I still had things to say.'

'You had said quite enough,' Rico returned imperturbably, deep eyes flat and emotionless. 'If you behave yourself, I'll let you ring again later.'

'If I behave.'

Bitterly she echoed his use of the word, wishing she dared rebel but knowing that she would be risking retribution if she tried any such foolishness.

'And I suppose that by "behaving", you mean doing exactly as you say?'

Those impressive shoulders under the fine tailoring lifted in a shrug of supreme indifference.

'You can try doing otherwise,' he declared flatly. 'And see where it gets you. But, frankly, I would advise against it.'

It was his calmness that got to her. The cold, obsidian darkness of his eyes, the totally emotionless tone in which he had spoken, the complete lack of expression in the words he had used, all added up to an appearance of total carelessness. But a creeping sensation running down her spine warned her that she would be a fool to believe it in any way.

Ricardo Valeron was in complete charge of this situation, and what he said went. His hands were on the reins, controlling every movement, every development, and she could kick and scream as hard as she liked; it would be to no avail. She had about as much power over her own future as a marionette that moves only according to the whim of the puppeteer who pulls the strings.

But that didn't mean she was about to lie down and let him walk all over her.

'I don't know what you think you're going to gain by all this! From where I stand you're hardly making a very good job of this kidnapping business.'

'And, as we've already established, you are the expert in such things.'

The way that beautiful mouth twitched faintly at one corner as Rico fought against the impulse to give into his amusement was almost her undoing. She couldn't bear the thought that he was laughing at her; that he wasn't even taking her seriously.

'There are laws against such things in this country!' she declared furiously. 'You can be prosecuted—imprisoned! I believe there's even a possible life sentence if you're found guilty.'

That hint of a smile grew, putting a devilishly taunting gleam into the depths of those black coffee eyes.

'Ah, but you see, Felicity, *querida*, no court in the world would possibly convict me on this.'

'Of course they will! They'll have to!'

Her temper ran away with her, blinding her to the possible dangers of her impulsive words.

'I'll give evidence against you—I—I'll even bring a private prosecution, if I have to. I'll make sure you pay for this!'

'You can try, *gatita*, but I doubt if you'd succeed. After all, why should any court want to hand out a life sentence to a man who has already taken on such a thing quite willingly?'

'A man who has *what*?'

Felicity could only shake her head in confusion, her grey eyes clouded with incomprehension.

'You're not making any sense! Just what are you talking about?'

'It's quite simple, *gatita*.'

Rico's voice was a rich purr of triumph, the gleam in his eyes brightening as verbally he moved in for the kill.

'What is it you say? For better for worse, for richer for poorer…until death do us part.'

'You've really lost me now.'

Was the man totally off his head? She had thought things couldn't get any worse but now it seemed that she was involved with a complete maniac.

'Just what have the words of the marriage service to do with anything?'

'They have everything to do with this, *mi ángel*. There are some who would say that marriage itself is a life sentence, and certainly no court on earth would condemn a man for wanting to run away with his promised bride.'

'His…'

Felicity's head was swimming, her stomach twisting in panic. Her throat was painfully dry and she had to swallow hard to relieve the constriction in it before she could even try to speak.

'I'm not going to marry you! No one would ever believe that!' she croaked unevenly.

'Oh, but they already do believe it,' Rico assured her, the conviction in his eyes and his voice turning her blood to ice and leaching all the colour from her face. 'Why do you think your father was so pleased with life?'

'No!'

Her mind was just one wild scream of protest but still the only sound that she could force from her throat was a raw, husky whisper.

'Yes,' Rico insisted with soft menace. 'Oh, yes. Everyone, all your family and friends who gathered in the cathedral think that you left poor Edward standing at the altar because you had fallen madly in love with someone else and wanted to be with him.'

'And that someone else is *you*?'

She couldn't smooth the horror from her voice, a horror that doubled, trebled in strength as Rico inclined his proud dark head in nonchalant agreement.

'But why should they think that? What on earth would make them believe—?'

'They believe it because you told them. Because that was what was in the message you sent—'

'The message *you* sent!' Felicity broke in on him, her voice shaking with horror. 'You said that! You told the lie! I never...'

He didn't even have the grace to look shamefaced. Instead he simply regarded her with that cool, unmoving stare, those luxurious lashes looking impossibly long around the darkness of his eyes.

'It doesn't matter who said what, *querida*,' he drawled

with slow insolence. 'What matters is what everyone believes, and they all believe what they've been told. No one will be setting the police on our trail. No one will be coming after us now, or at any other time in the future. Why should they when they think that all we want is to be alone together?'

Shock and consternation froze her tongue in her mouth. She couldn't force herself to form a single word, her brain too numb to collect together any rational thoughts. She longed to be able to scream at him, to yell defiance straight into his watchful face, to tell him she didn't believe…

But everything about him told her that he had spoken nothing but the truth. That calm frighteningly relaxed demeanour, the controlled delivery of his words revealed an unshakeable conviction of everything he had said.

And so she could only stand frozen to the spot and watch transfixed as he slid one long-fingered hand into the pocket of his trousers and pulled out a jingling keying.

The faint rasp of metal on metal as he pushed a key into the lock on the door, the click as he turned it, making it secure, scraped over the tightly drawn nerves that were too close to the surface of her skin, making her shiver miserably.

'So you see, sweet Felicity, we might as well make ourselves comfortable, because it looks as if there will only be the two of us here for the rest of the night.'

Casually he tossed the bunch of keys up into the air, catching them one-handed as they fell back down, and Felicity was so painfully on edge that when he did so she actually flinched back sharply as if afraid of something lurking in the shadows.

'As a matter of fact,' Rico continued still in that lazily drawling tone, 'it's obvious it will be just you and me for the foreseeable future. And that is exactly the way I want it to be.'

CHAPTER SIX

THE sun was high in a bright, cloudless sky before Felicity even stirred, the brilliance of the day almost blinding her as she reluctantly opened her heavy eyes and peered around her. It had taken her a long, long time to fall asleep last night, and now the clinging, heavy strands of drowsiness still lingered like sticky spiders' webs, adhering to her thoughts and dulling them painfully.

For a few long, welcome seconds she actually didn't recall where she was and stared in blank incomprehension at a room she didn't recognise. It certainly wasn't the bedroom at Highson House where she had been expecting to find herself in on the morning after her wedding.

But then her memory returned and with it a stream of appalling, unwelcome images that flooded into her mind, swamping her thoughts and making her head drop back against the pillow again with a groan of rejection and despair.

'Ricardo Valeron!'

The sound of his name was like an imprecation on her lips, driven from them by a sense of impotent fury and dejection.

'Rico the louse Valeron! Rico damn-him-to-hell's-horrors rotten Valeron!'

There was a whole new sense of satisfaction to be gained from creating abusive titles for the man who had brought her here. Stringing them together in a litany of hatred, while it actually achieved nothing positive at least it made her feel a little better for venting the force of her feelings.

'Rico the—'

'Yes?'

The response came so suddenly that Felicity actually started up in bed, her wild-eyed gaze going to the doorway and focussing apprehensively on Rico's tall, strong form, trying to gauge his mood.

But it was impossible to read anything from the inscrutable set of his hard features, the way the brilliant dark eyes were hooded and unrevealing. Seeing him, Felicity couldn't hold back a groan of disappointment.

'I had thought that you were just a dream.'

A slow smile curled Rico's beautiful mouth, making her heart kick sharply in her chest.

'I dreamed of you too, *querida*,' he drawled softly, ebony eyes sweeping over her from the top of her ruffled blonde head and down her sleep-warmed face, lingering briefly, sensually on her wide, cloudy grey eyes before dropping to the fullness of her mouth.

Oh, yes, he'd dreamed of her, Rico remembered, fighting the erotic kick his body gave him. He'd dreamed of that rose-coloured mouth and the pleasure it could bring, the soft caress of it on his flesh, until his body had overheated and he'd woken, aching, throbbing, his pulse racing and his skin slick with sweat.

After that it had proved almost impossible to get back to sleep for the rest of the night. He had lain awake for hours imagining her here in this bed, in the room next to his, his ears sensitive to even the slightest sound she made.

But his imaginings hadn't even come close to the delights of reality.

'I never said I dreamed *of* you!' Felicity protested indignantly, struggling to sit back against the pillows and sweeping a silken swathe of soft blonde hair back out of her eyes. 'And if I had, believe me, it would have been such a nightmare that it would have had me screaming in a panic.'

Had she sounded too vehement? Would those observant

bitter chocolate eyes see past the shield she had tried to put up between his probing gaze and her feelings and realise that she was struggling to convince herself almost as much as—if not more than—him?

'I would have woken up the whole house.'

'But as there is no one here but the two of us, that would hardly have mattered.'

Rico strolled into the room and came to sit on the end of the bed, making Felicity curl her legs up rapidly to avoid any contact with his lean body, even through the softness of the luxurious duvet that covered her.

'And I would have been only too happy to come and rescue you from your nightmares and soothe you back to sleep in my arms.'

'Oh, I'll bet you would!' Felicity growled ungraciously, fighting the unwanted direction of her thoughts.

It was impossible not to let her eyes follow the long, lean lines of muscle in the smoothly olive-skinned arms exposed by the short sleeves of his navy polo shirt and imagine them being wrapped around her, their strength holding her close. The neck of the shirt was unbuttoned, opening to reveal just enough honeyed golden skin to tease and tantalise her sexually awakened senses. Heat licked along her veins, drying her mouth and making her pulse thud heavily.

'But of course sleep would not be the first thing on my mind.'

'No?'

Felicity's attempt at sarcastic disbelief was ruined by the way that the dryness of her throat turned the word into an embarrassing croak that revealed so much about her mental state, it sent hot colour flooding into her cheeks.

'You do surprise me!'

'And it would not be on your mind either,' he continued imperturbably, ignoring the cynicism of her comment. 'Oh, you might fight the idea at first—just a little—just for form's sake. But it would all be nothing but a pretence.'

'You egotistical pig!'

Fiery rejection of his words flared in her grey eyes, her chin coming up sharply as she glared into his arrogant dark face.

'You really think that all you'd have to do is click your fingers and any woman would come running like some panting little lap dog just waiting for the touch of its master's hand?'

'Oh, no, *gatita*...'

Something in Rico's smile scraped a protective layer away from Felicity's skin, leaving it raw and vulnerable.

'For one thing, when you are around, I do not want *any* woman. I just want one—and only one. And I'm sure I don't need to tell you who she is.'

He didn't have to say a word. It was there in the darkness of his eyes, in the way they were fixed on her face. Everything about him declared without words just what was in his mind. The heady atmosphere of desire seemed to permeate the air of the room.

And the problem was that she felt it too. Even just sitting here like this, her skin was prickling with awareness, her thoughts whirling. She inhaled the warm, clean scent of his body with every breath she took in and her wanton senses clamoured for something more than just the small pleasures of simply observing, which was all she dared allow them.

'When you are in the room I am only aware of you. There could be a hundred other women present and I would see none of them. There would only be you...'

'And am I supposed to be flattered by that?'

Desperately she used aggression as a self-defence mechanism. She didn't want to listen to his seductive tone, was terrified of being swayed by his cajolery, but in spite of herself the extravagant compliments had made her heart flutter betrayingly.

'Not flattered, no.'

Rico shook his dark head, his smile fading, leaving behind a seriousness she didn't dare even think to doubt.

'Believe me, I do not flatter.'

His accent had deepened on the words, turning them into a tigerishly sensual purr that stroked over the mental feathers his earlier comments had ruffled.

'I simply state a fact—and that fact is that you are a beautiful woman—the most beautiful woman it has ever been my experience to know. I only have to look at you to want you. And you feel the same about me.'

'No...'

In her turn Felicity shook her head, willing herself to look away, to break the hold he had on her. But even as her mind screamed instructions her body refused to obey. Her eyes lingered on the handsome, intensely male figure before her.

'No,' she tried again, more successfully this time.

'Si!' Rico insisted forcefully, dismissing her protest with a flick of his hand. 'You know it's the truth. With you I would not even need to click my fingers. With you I can just sit back and wait...'

Suiting actions to the words, he relaxed back against the end of the bed, lounging with indolent elegance on the downy quilt, long, long legs in tight denim jeans coming dangerously close to her own. A light in his eyes challenged her to deny his arrogant assertion, a provocation she was determined to take up.

'Then you'll have a very long wait indeed,' she declared furiously. 'Hell would freeze over before I'd let you touch me again!'

'Really, my sweet Felicity.. '

Rico shook his head in mock reproach, black coffee eyes gleaming through thick, lushly curling lashes.

'You really must stop throwing out these threats that you can't make good. Last night you said you would kill me if I so much as touched you; this morning you are like a little wild cat, spitting and hissing in a pretence of fury...'

'It's not a *pretence*!' she spluttered, her fury increasing a hundredfold as she saw one dark straight brow lift in cynical questioning. 'I am *not joking*!'

'And neither am I, *mi ángel*,' he assured her, the soft murmur of the words threaded through with a darker, deeper undertone that made her shiver involuntarily, her toes curling nervously under the pale blue cotton. 'I have never been more deadly serious in my life.'

The dark-eyed gaze held her smoky grey eyes with a magnetic intensity, keeping her transfixed so that no matter how she longed to tear her eyes away, to look anywhere but into the depths of his, she couldn't manage it. She could only sit there, mesmerised by the magnetic force of his presence and the low, husky sound of his voice as it coiled round her like the scent of incense, weaving a hypnotic spell to hold her prisoner without any effort.

'You know this is there between us, so why try to deny it? Why try to fight something we both want?'

The light covering of the quilt was becoming far too hot for Felicity to bear, her skin burning and sensitive even to the slightest touch of Rico's scorching gaze. She longed to toss aside the bedcovers in an attempt to cool her racing pulse but the recollection that she was only wearing a loose white tee-shirt, provided by Rico in the place of sleepwear the previous night, made her determined to grit her teeth and endure the discomfort that was more mental than physical.

'I don't want it!'

'No, *querida*?'

Rico's tone was frankly sceptical.

'I think in this case I know you better than you know yourself. Remember, I held you in my arms last night. I kissed you and caressed you and felt your response to those kisses—the way you went wild for my touch.'

Felicity tried once more to deny what he was saying but he froze her shake of her head with one flashing glance from those deep brown eyes.

'I know that you want more—that you are still as hungry for me as I am for you. But I also know that you are a coward. That you do not dare to admit your need...'

'A coward? How dare you? I'll show you who's a coward!'

Incensed by his goading tone, the gleam of contempt in the brilliant dark eyes, she threw caution to the wind, flinging back the quilt as she launched herself at him in a physical expression of her mental fury.

'How *dare*...?'

Too late she realised just what she had done, the danger in which her unthinking reaction had placed her.

She was lying half across the hard male body, the firm wall of his chest against her breasts, the powerful length of his legs beneath hers. And the already barely adequate covering of the white tee-shirt had rucked up around her waist, exposing embarrassing amounts of her own slim pale legs, the soft curves of her buttocks.

As Felicity froze in horror, shock depriving her of the power of speech or movement, Rico tilted his dark head to look down into her wide, appalled grey eyes.

'Do you know, *gatita*, I really think you should keep that shirt. It looks so much more appealing on you than it ever did on me.'

If the truth was told, the combination of the soft, clinging material and the slim, curving lines of her body beneath it had lit a fire in his senses that had heated his blood, making his heart thud in a heavy languorous pulse all the time they had been talking.

But then she had moved and that warmth had flared from sensuous smoulder to raging conflagration in the space of a heartbeat. Every inch of him had tightened in hungry craving, his body growing hard and yearning in a second, totally beyond his control. And as if that wasn't bad enough he now had to endure having the soft weight of her lying across him, her breasts crushed against his chest, her legs tangled with his. At his sides his hands clenched over the blue quilt, fighting against the impulse—the *need*—to reach out and touch the soft flesh she had so recklessly exposed to his darkened gaze.

'Felicity...' was all he could manage, his voice roughened and husky as if his throat had dried in the heat that had spread through every cell in his body.

There it was again, Felicity thought hazily. That sensuous, tantalisingly accented drawl that turned her name into an exotic alien sound.

Fayleeseetay.

The four syllables swirled round her head like an enchanter's incantation. *Fayleeseetay* was her, and yet someone else entirely. Someone unknown and alluring, with a lifestyle that was much more colourful and glamorous than her own matter of fact existence. Someone suited to be the partner of this wicked, dangerous, but nevertheless disturbingly enthralling brigand of a man. A bandit with dark eyes and...

No! Looking into his eyes was dangerous. It was taking a risk that she couldn't afford. It meant seeing how those already dark eyes had become even more heavy-lidded and impenetrable behind the lush curtain of jet-black lashes.

It meant remembering... Remembering how last night he had looked into her face in just this way. And how then the pupils of those stunning eyes had expanded until there was no trace of any coffee-brown, other than the tiny rim at the outermost edge of the iris, faintly outlining the black. And that darkness had told its own story, sending a shiver down her spine with its revelation of deep, fierce desire, its promise of passion to come.

It meant remembering how his touch had felt on her skin, feeling the ache of wanting start up again in spite of her efforts to wipe it from her mind.

And his mouth was so close to hers that it was impossible not to recall the pressure of it against her own. The way it had tasted when he had kissed her so forcefully last night. Kisses that were etched on to her memory. Kisses that she longed to feel again.

'Rico...' she managed chokingly.

She wasn't sure who moved first, whether his proud dark head lowered or her own lifted to his. Or perhaps they both moved together, both driven by the same urgent impulse, the same burning primal need that would allow no restraint.

His kiss was hard and demanding and sure. Sure of her response. Sure of his own welcome. And at first that arrogant confidence was so shocking that just for a second she fought against it, resisting the sensuous invasion of his tongue, trying to close her mouth against it.

But in the space of one, wild, unsteady heartbeat her resistance crumbled and she found herself opening to him, succumbing to the hot, melting sensation that swamped her mind, destroying all rational thought. She was only conscious of two things—this man and his strength holding her, and the heavy, honeyed pulse of need that set up at the most feminine centre of her being.

'Felicity, *belleza*!'

It was a raw, husky murmur against her skin as his mouth left hers to press hard, forceful kisses over her face, on her cheeks, her temples, on her weakly closed lids. She let herself be hauled up against him, the rough material of his jeans harsh against the tender skin of her legs. The tee-shirt she wore was pushed even higher, bunching around her waist, leaving her naked below.

'I think we can dispense with this,' Rico growled, pulling it up and off her in one smooth movement. An action she did nothing to resist but instead helped him as much as she could, effecting a small, eager little wriggle that effectively freed her from the last clinging folds of the inadequate garment.

'You too…'

Her own voice sounded as husky and shaken as his had and her fingers were unsteady as they fumbled the navy shirt free from the leather belt at his waist and pushed it aside. Every sense in her body was hungry for him, for the sight of the olive smoothness of his skin, for the feel of the strong, pulsing life of his body. All around her was the warm, clean scent of him, and as she pressed her lips to his chest, feeling the taut muscles bunch and tense under her caress, the ragged, uneven sound of his breathing was the only sound that she could hear.

'*Madre de Dios!*' he muttered thickly, his long body twisting sharply so that instead of being on top of him she was now underneath, lying on her back and being hoisted against the pillows, crushed into the yielding softness of the mattress by the dominant strength of his body.

Blindly she reached for him again, wanting to tangle her nerveless fingers in the silken black strands of his hair, draw his mouth down to hers again for another of those potent, mind-blowing kisses. But Rico had other ideas, rearing up slightly and arching away for her, deep brown eyes burning with carnal hunger as he subjected her pale, slim body to a slowly searing survey that licked over her exposed flesh with a touch of fire.

Hot, hard hands smoothed her skin, shaping every curve, every contour, arranging her just so, with her head on the pillow, her fine blonde hair spread out all around it, her hands at her sides, her limbs straight and relaxed.

And when she was positioned exactly as he wanted her, he let his fingertips trail once more down the line of her body, making her writhe in sensual reaction beneath his touch.

'Rico…' she gasped, his lazy, indulgent approach warring with the fiery hunger he had awakened inside her.

But Rico simply shook his dark head, his dark-eyed gaze absorbed, intent on what he was doing.

'Wait, *gatita*,' he murmured softly. 'Take things slowly. The pleasure will be all the greater that way.'

Easing himself down in the bed, he lifted one slender leg and pressed the heat of his mouth to her foot, kissing it unhurriedly from the tip of her curling toes to the fine bones of her ankle, and then upwards, his hands following the same movement with soft, featherlight caresses.

Felicity's protests died to a murmur of pure delight as she lay submissive to his control of the situation. She had thought it was impossible for her body to awaken any more, to become even more responsive to the feel of this man's touch, the stroke of his lips along her skin. But wherever his hands or his mouth had been her skin burned with pleasure, leaving her feeling as if she had been bathing in the heat of a brilliant sun, every cell experiencing the glorious sensation of well-being.

Her breath caught in her throat, her limp body tensing momentarily as Rico's kisses brought that tormenting mouth to within an inch of the most intimate core of her being. But still he moved slowly upwards, kissing his way over her quivering stomach, pausing momentarily to let his tongue slide around and briefly dip into the shallow dimple of her navel, and then continuing inching progress upwards.

Her breasts were subjected to the same sensual torment. Rico's mouth kissed its way infinitesimally up each soft, curving slope before pausing at the crest to flick a warm, moist tongue around and around the pouting nipple until it hardened with desire. Only when she was gasping in wordless protest at the torture of waiting he was imposing on her did he take pity on her yearning body and capture one swollen nub, drawing it into the heat of his mouth and suckling hard.

'Rico!'

His name was all that she was capable of as her body clenched in violent response to the savage sting of pleasure that burned its way along every nerve, pooling in a flood of liquid heat at the most intimate point between her legs.

'Rico, *please*!'

And now it seemed that at last the inhuman patience that Rico had shown was exhausted. The whole tempo of his lovemaking changed, slow control giving way to a hungry impatience that matched and outstripped her own. Hands clumsy with desire, he fumbled with his belt, yanking the buckle open. For a moment he cursed in soft Spanish as the zip on his jeans stuck briefly, but then it was free and seconds later the last of his remaining clothing had been kicked off, discarded wildly onto the floor.

'Now…' he rasped harshly, looking deep into her wide, dazed grey eyes. 'Now I will love you properly.'

Above the flare of heated colour high on his cheekbones his eyes were like black coals, blazing in the firestorm of passion, burning away all restraint.

'*Now*…' he muttered again, roughly pushing her legs apart and sliding his own powerful hair-roughened limbs between them.

'Now…' Felicity echoed, meeting and matching the hard hot force of his desire all the way.

She lifted her hips to meet the thrust of his possession, a sigh of mindless pleasure, of completion, escaping her as she felt the full force of his arousal fill her in one fierce uncontrolled movement. But that sigh turned to wild cries of delight, small at first, but growing to a sharp crescendo as each slide and twist of his powerful body, each new refinement of the pagan throbbing pace of his lovemaking roused her to fever pitch in seconds. She was mindless, out of control, able only to follow where he led.

Her pulse was a hot, heavy pounding inside her head, her body matching its demanding rhythm as together they moved to higher, sharper peaks of pleasure. And those pleasures took them further and further into a dark heated world of passion from which there was only one escape. And in the final seconds as the waves of ecstasy broke over her Felicity clutched at the muscled strength of Rico's shoulders, clinging on to the one hard fact of reality in a world in which all that she was seemed to be splintering about her.

But then the erotic pressure inside her exploded into a blaze of whirling stars and she lost herself completely.

CHAPTER SEVEN

WHAT the hell had he done?

Rico woke to a rush of realisation that swamped him like a forceful tidal wave.

What in the name of God had he been thinking of? Had he lost all common sense? Had the past twenty-four hours drained every last drop of sanity from his mind?

What was he? A mature, developed adult or some hormone-driven adolescent whose every motivation originated below his waist?

Making every effort to avoid any further physical contact with the woman sleeping beside him in the bed, he turned until he was lying on his back. Pushing both hands roughly through the sleek blackness of his hair he stared up at the ceiling, his breath leaving him in a sigh of disbelief at his own foolishness.

He hadn't wanted any part of this at the beginning. Maria had made her own bed; she would have to lie in it. It was time that she learned that everyone made mistakes. And mistakes had consequences.

Everyone made mistakes!

The thought was like a dash of cold water in his face, driving away the last remaining shadows of sleep and bringing his mind fully wide awake. Uncomfortably so. Suddenly too restless to lie still any more, he flung back the quilt and got out of bed. Snatching up his jeans and underwear from where they lay in a crumpled heap on the floor, he pulled them on swiftly, still yanking up the zip as he moved to stare out of the window at the far side of the room.

Wasn't what he had just done every bit as much of a mistake as Maria's unthinking behaviour had been? And what in the name of heaven was he going to do if *his* mistake resulted in the same sort of consequences as his half-sister's had?

'You fool!' he berated himself out loud, slamming one hand hard against the wall in a gesture of impotent fury. 'You damn, stupid fool!'

Some unexpected sound penetrated the deep, drugging sleep into which sheer exhaustion had finally driven Felicity, making her stir slightly in the bed, frowning faintly in confusion.

Even before her eyes opened she became aware of the space beside her, the cooling sheets where the last time she had been capable of any sort of conscious thought there had been the hard, warm strength of a very male body.

Rico's body.

Reality flooded back with a shock that jerked her upright, blonde hair wildly tousled, grey eyes clouded with shocked despair at the situation in which she found herself.

Oh, *what* had she done! How could she possibly have let this happen? How could the situation have got so completely out of hand? How could she...

'Good afternoon, Señorita Hamilton.'

The quiet voice, edged with a note she couldn't interpret, came from by the window, bringing her head round in a rush. The sun was so brilliant that she had to narrow her eyes, squinting slightly, before she could make out exactly where he was, but even then he was still just a dark silhouette etched against it.

'Is it really that late?'

She didn't really need to ask. The light that poured into the room, casting a shadow of Rico's tall, lean body across the rich blue carpet was so very different from the one that had woken her earlier that day.

'Late enough,' he returned laconically. 'We were—occupied for quite some time.'

The reminder stung, making hot colour suffuse her whole body at the memory of just how 'occupied' they had been. That first wild coming together had only satisfied them both for a short time. It hadn't been long before the shuddering aftershocks of passion had subsided into a languid peace, a peace that had soon been broken by the slow dawning of a new phase of desire. And in the space of a couple of heartbeats the hunger had gripped them again, making them reach for each other in mutual need.

'I—fell asleep...' she managed shakily, lifting a faintly unsteady hand to sweep back the tangle of blonde hair that had fallen forward over her eyes. She regretted the action immediately as the brush of her arm against her breast brought home to her that she was still as completely naked as the moment she had fallen asleep in Rico's arms.

Instinctively she clutched at the bedclothes, wanting to pull them up over her exposed body, but just at that moment Rico moved out of the direct path of the sunlight. For the first time she could see his face clearly and the expression of burning scorn deep in the dark eyes froze her actions.

She could almost read his mind, hear the cynical comment that it was way too late for any degree of modesty clearly forming on his lips. She would do anything rather than give him the opportunity to use it, she told herself, fierce pride forcing her to regard him from behind a mask of cold indifference that she prayed he would see as genuine.

'You look as bad as I feel,' he declared roughly, pushing his hands deep into the pockets of his jeans and standing, bare feet planted firmly apart, shoulders slightly hunched, exactly halfway between her and the door. 'Very definitely the morning after the night before, except that in our case it should really be the afternoon after the morning before.'

'Is that a polite way of trying to tell me that this shouldn't have happened?'

To her intense relief some of the control she was imposing over her body had its effect on her voice as well. She sounded every bit as cool and indifferent as she would have wished.

'We both know it shouldn't have happened.'

If she had been cool, then Rico was positively glacial.

'This was a mistake from start to finish and one I have no intention of repeating.'

'I don't remember offering you the opportunity to do so!' Felicity retorted tartly. 'I regret what happened every bit as much as—'

'Oh, I never said I *regretted* it,' Rico inserted smoothly, stopping her dead. 'There's not a man alive who could ever regret an experience like that.'

The ebony gazed dropped to the bed, surveying the crumpled disorder of the sheet and duvet for a long second before it flicked back up to her stunned face. And the look in those brilliant dark eyes made her skin veer from burning heat to icy cold and back again in the space of a second, making her feel as if she was in the grip of an unpleasant fever.

'But it complicates things unnecessarily, and that is something I can do without.'

'Complicates…?'

It was all Felicity could manage, her thoughts reeling in shock. Was that all she was to him? A complication? It was shocking how much it hurt.

'Oh, of course!' she murmured bitterly. 'You wouldn't want to mess up your clever little plan with something as untidy as feelings.'

'Feelings?' Rico sounded as if he didn't even understand what the word meant. 'Who brought feelings into this?'

'Well, not you, that's for sure!'

She wouldn't—couldn't—let him see what he was doing to her. She mustn't let him see how every word he spoke stabbed further into her feelings, slicing them into tiny, bleeding pieces. And the worst thing was that she couldn't see why it should hurt quite so much.

After all, Rico was nothing to her—he was little more than a stranger. A man she had only known for barely twenty-four hours. A man who had already proved himself capable of taking a cold-blooded revenge on someone he hated, for whatever reason, and had been prepared to use her as part of that plan. She knew what he was like so this new evidence of his callous heartlessness should not have come as such a shock. She should have expected it all along, armoured her feelings against it.

But somehow she couldn't even convince herself that it was that simple.

'And not me,' she continued, the turmoil of feelings deep inside adding an extra bite to her words. 'Men aren't the only ones who can enjoy sex for its own sake—for just the simple pleasure of it.'

He flinched. He actually flinched, just for a second, as if in distaste at her words. The hypocrisy of his reaction incensed her further, fury driving all thoughts of caution from her mind.

'Does that shock you? Oh, come now, darling...'

She'd never thought of herself as an actress but somehow she dragged up enough strength to perform the role she'd set herself with something close to conviction. Her chin came up determinedly, grey eyes flashing defiance, and her voice dripped acid as she goaded him deliberately.

'Have you never heard the saying that what's sauce for the goose is sauce for the gander? This is the twenty-first century, after all. Women have been liberated for decades and we enjoy all the same freedoms that you men have. The double standard is dead and gone and if you don't like it, well—tough.'

'And why should I not like it?' Rico demanded, cutting her off in mid flow. 'If you must know, it suits me fine that you feel that way. At least now I know that I'm not likely to be troubled by any unwanted emotions on your part. That when this is over we can go our separate ways without a second thought.'

And he wouldn't have to live with the reproaches of an uncomfortable conscience. Maria had warned him that this woman was no angel, but a calculating opportunist who had seen marrying Edward Venables as the quick route to a fortune and a place in society. And hadn't his own investigator said much the same in the reports he had submitted? Reports that detailed this Felicity's regular trips to a seedy night-club where she spent long, probably drunken evenings, never emerging until the early hours of the following morning.

He had let himself forget about those evenings when he had been at the mercy of his clamouring sex, but he knew differently now. Felicity's outburst had taught him how wrong he had been to let himself be blinded by a beautiful face, distracted by the undeniable charms of her body. It was a lesson he had needed, but one he would now never forget.

'After all, we're both adults.'

'Of course.'

Felicity's throat ached from the effort she was making to keep her voice even and firm. She was painfully aware of the fact that the rigid control she needed made it sound even harder and more brittle than ever. But the way she felt inside was in complete contrast to the way she sounded. She couldn't stay in bed like this. It made her feel too defenceless and vulnerable sitting there while Rico towered over her, big and dark and infinitely disturbing. Defenceless enough to actually be prepared to expose herself to his cold-eyed scrutiny when she forced herself to fling back the covers and stand up.

'We're both grown up and understand that sometimes sex can do some very strange things to otherwise reasonably intelligent people.'

Spotting the white tee-shirt that Rico had stripped from her body with such impatience—a lifetime ago, it seemed— she stalked over to where it lay on the floor and picked it up. Much as she longed to huddle herself into it in a frantic rush, she forced herself to take her time, knowing that any haste would not escape those coolly observant brown eyes and would be interpreted as a sign of the weakness she couldn't afford to show.

With the protective barrier of the soft cotton between herself and the burning dark gaze, she felt stronger, more confident. So much so that she even managed to flash a coolly supercilious smile in the direction of Rico's darkly brooding face.

'It can push you into the arms of the most unsuitable people, drive you wild with passion for someone that you hate the sight of when you wake up again the next morning. We've all had one-night stands that we're embarrassed by afterwards.'

At least she assumed that he had. The only experience she had to go on was one sweet, almost childlike relationship that had had a terrible ending. She had never had a one-night stand with anyone in her life.

'How very mature of you to see it that way.'

Rico's tone implied the exact opposite of his words.

'So is that what we've had—a one-night stand?' he continued.

'Near enough—except that in our case, I suppose, strictly

speaking it was a one-morning stand, but we won't quibble
about words.'

'Of course not.' The black cynicism of his tone made
her wince. 'And I presume that as mature adults we now
forget that it ever happened?'

Oh, if only they could! If only it *had* never happened!

'I think that would be best,' she said instead.

Forget! Rico almost laughed out loud. He had as much
chance of not remembering the morning he'd just spent as
of forgetting his own name. And even if his mind tried to
push away thoughts of the heated lovemaking, the intense
pleasure, his body refused to follow suit. He might have
thought that once Felicity was dressed, if only in the skimp-
ily inadequate tee-shirt, then it would be easier to drive the
recollection of that glorious body from his mind. But instead it made matters worse.

Every movement she made tugged the soft material
against the curves he had caressed only so recently. Even
though it had been made in his size, and there was much
more room for her slender figure than there had ever been
for his bulkier frame, the shirt still revealed expanses of
the soft creamy flesh on which he had planted so many
heated kisses during the long, passion-filled morning. And
there was something almost shockingly intimate about the
realisation that she was wearing something that only days
before had covered his own flesh. His body clenched with
hunger just at the thought.

'So we carry on as before?' he asked.

'I think that would be best.. '

Her smile was brief, tight, and blatantly insincere.

What would be best *for him* was that he should grab her,
swing her up into his arms as he had the day before, carry
her over to that bed and strip that sexy piece of nothing
she was wearing from her...

Dios! No! Wrenching his thoughts back under control,

he switched on a smile that matched hers for hypocrisy. He'd never been rejected by a woman in quite this way before—in fact, he'd never been rejected at all, full stop. It was an experience he wasn't enjoying and the feeling made him want to lash out, at least verbally.

'I have to admit that when I decided on this course of action I hadn't realised quite how effective it would be. I knew Venables would be furious at losing his bride, but I'd never reckoned on just how much he would be missing. If that's the way you perform for him in bed, *querida*, it's no wonder he wanted to rush the wedding through so fast.'

Felicity had thought that it was impossible for her mental state to get any worse. That nothing Rico could do or say would make her feel any more degraded and used than she did already. But the callous indifference with which he had tossed a reminder of why she was here straight into her face was more painful than if his words had been an actual assault.

'And is that the only reason that you…you bedded me?'

For the life of her she couldn't force her tongue to form the phrase 'made love to me'. It was one that had no possible relevance to what had happened between her and Rico. That had been sex, pure and simple—though there had been nothing *pure* about the way this hateful man had behaved.

'Was it all just to get back at Edward for whatever you believe he's done to you?'

'Oh, no, *querida*.'

Rico's smile was demonic, the cold gleam in his eyes making her shiver just to see it.

'Getting back at Venables wasn't all there was to it. There was a great deal of pleasure for me in the experience. In fact, it's one I would very much like to repeat in the future.'

'Well, don't fool yourself into dreaming that you'll ever get the chance. Once was more than enough for me...'

She accompanied her words with a delicate shudder that was more eloquently damning than any longer tirade could ever be.

'And now if you don't mind I'd very much like to get washed—I'm feeling decidedly grubby.'

And she wanted to wash away every trace of his touch, the scent of his body from her skin, the last lingering evidence of his lovemaking. She didn't have to put the feeling into words. It was there in the cold set of her face, the ice that made her eyes look as cold as the sea on a bleak day in deep midwinter.

'Be my guest.'

Lazily he strolled round the room, picking up his discarded shirt, his socks and shoes. He would leave in his own time, and there was no way he was going to let her obvious impatience, the furious sparks in those wide grey eyes, rush him into doing anything before he was ready.

'I'll make us both a coffee and something to eat. I reckon we could do with a meal, seeing as we haven't eaten all day.'

It would probably stick in her throat, choking her, if she had to sit opposite him and eat anything. Her stomach heaved at the thought. But once again she managed to flash that tight, brittle smile in his direction, though she couldn't bring herself to meet those deep ebony eyes.

'Fine. You do that. And then perhaps you'll be prepared to keep your promise.'

'Promise?' His quick frown revealed his lack of comprehension. 'I don't recall...'

'You said that if I didn't do anything stupid, like trying to escape during the night, then you would let me go this morning—today,' she amended belatedly, painfully aware of the fact that it was already well past noon.

It was the only reason she had stayed in her room overnight and hadn't even tried wandering the house, looking for a way of escape. Once she'd discarded the idea of climbing out of her bedroom window, that was. Looking out and realising just how high up it was, the distance she would fall if she slipped, had been enough to make her shudder.

'I made no promise. I simply said that if things had gone according to plan I would consider letting you go.'

'But surely things have? Haven't they?'

The nonchalant shrug that lifted those powerfully muscled shoulders implied supreme indifference to her question.

'I have no idea,' he drawled sardonically. 'I haven't had time to check. I was—too busy elsewhere.'

Once more those dark eyes drifted towards the bed; the sudden slight softening of his expression, the almost nostalgic smile, proved positively the last straw.

'Then check, damn you!' she exploded. 'I want to get out of here and the sooner the better.'

And unable to bear his company any longer she turned on her heel and stalked swiftly into the en suite bathroom, slamming the door behind her and locking it firmly.

CHAPTER EIGHT

FELICITY pushed open the door to the kitchen and peered warily inside. She was not at all sure what sort of mood Rico would be in after the way she had left him upstairs.

He had been gone from her room by the time she'd got out of the shower. And that was something she'd been very thankful for. After all that had happened she didn't at all relish the prospect of having to face him again with only a pale blue towel wrapped round her.

But the room had been empty and silent, surprisingly with the bed carefully made, the pillows fluffed up and the duvet smoothed out so that no evidence remained of anything that had happened there that morning.

If only she could smooth out her memories and her life quite that easily, Felicity thought now, her nerves twisting themselves into agonising knots as Rico turned from where he stood by the stove and the dark eyes flicked over her in swift appraisal.

'I was beginning to wonder where you were,' he said surprisingly evenly. 'I thought you'd got lost on the way down.'

'Or that I jumped from a window, perhaps, and tried to escape? I thought about it, believe me. I tried every door I could find as well.'

Unexpectedly Rico grinned.

'I knew you would. That's why I made sure everything was secure before you came down. And in case you're wondering where the keys are...'

One hand patted the front pocket of his jeans creating a faint metallic jingle.

Well, if there was one place the keys were absolutely safe it was there, Felicity thought, her mouth twisting wryly. She certainly wasn't prepared to go hunting in that pocket for them. When her mind showed an unfortunate tendency to drift off on to thoughts of the moments earlier when her fingers had traced the muscles in that most intimate spot, the way his skin had felt like hot satin, she wrenched them back mercilessly, forcing herself to concentrate on the present.

'What would you like to drink? Coffee?'

Perhaps a hot drink would warm her, ease some of the cold tension that gripped her in spite of the heat of the day.

'I'll make it.'

'No, you sit down, I'll do it—Felicity…' he added emphatically when she still hesitated. 'Sit down! You can relax; I'm not going to poison you.'

'Not poison perhaps, but how do I know you're not going to slip something into my drink?'

'*Madre de Dios!*' Rico exploded, raking both hands through the dark sleekness of his hair. 'I told you, that was a one-off—an emergency measure. You are quite safe.'

The look Felicity turned on him was frankly sceptical. The word 'safe' and Rico Valeron were two things that just didn't go together, at least not where she was concerned. But one thing she had been forced to realise over the past twenty-four hours was that the emotional danger she was in from this man was far, far greater than any physical fear she might feel.

'You found the clean clothes, then,' Rico continued, spooning coffee into a filter machine and adding the water.

'Yes—thanks…'

She forced herself to say it. She had to wear something. The silk wedding dress was totally impractical, besides which she would have felt a total hypocrite to continue wearing it now that the prospect of her ever marrying Edward seemed as remote as the moon.

Last night Rico had offered her the loan of some of his own clothes—another tee-shirt and a pair of jeans—and she had gratefully accepted. And today, when she had finally emerged from the bathroom after scrubbing herself all over and standing under the hot spray for as long as possible, she had found another selection of shirts and tee-shirts neatly folded on a chair, waiting for her.

'The colour suits you, and the fit could be worse.'

'It is if I do this…' Felicity admitted, shaking out her arms so that the rolled-back sleeves of the deep turquoise shirt fell over her slender hands and flapped limply from the end of her fingers. 'And you could fit two of me inside here. I must look like a charity case—a kid dressed in big brother's hand-me-downs.'

'I like it,' Rico said, his voice suddenly dropping an octave, causing her dove-grey eyes to fly to his face in a rush. What she saw there made the colour leach from her face then almost immediately flood back into it again.

'Don't!' she said sharply. *'Don't!'*

'No. My apologies.'

Rico's tone was flat, unrevealing and abruptly he turned away, busying himself with taking mugs from a cupboard.

Would she ever get it right? Felicity wondered, subsiding uneasily into a nearby chair and forcing herself to concentrate on rolling her shirt sleeves back up to around her elbows. Would she ever get to the point where she could hold some sort of a conversation with this man without one or other of them stepping into the great, yawning traps that opened at their feet with every sentence?

But why should she even *want* to talk to him? Wouldn't she be much safer to keep a careful distance, hold herself aloof for whatever time longer she was forced to spend in his company? That way at least she had some hope of escaping from this situation with some degree of safety.

But the truth was that Rico fascinated and intrigued her. She was repelled by the heartless, cold-blooded way he had moved in on her life, throwing it into turmoil in order to further whatever private vendetta he had with Edward, but at the same time there were other aspects of him that tugged at her feelings, drawing her to him like a needle to a magnet. He was a man of contradictions; the two different sides to him were almost polar opposites, so that she couldn't tell which was the real Rico.

Last night, for example, just when she had been at her lowest point, when realisation of what had happened to her had finally hit home, knocking her for six and leaving her limp and miserable, he had suddenly switched from the ruthless brigand to become another man entirely.

She had been in the room he had shown her to, the room where she had slept last night. Rico had suggested that she make herself more comfortable and had left her there to change into the clothes he had provided for her.

It was the veil that had been her undoing. The veil and the delicate tracery of the tiara. Both had been professionally woven into place, fastened securely with innumerable pins, guaranteed to stay fixed for the entire day, and removing them had proved totally beyond her.

It was the last straw. Overcome with exhaustion and despair, she had given up even trying and had just sat there on the edge of the bed, staring unseeingly into the mirror before her.

That was where Rico had found her.

'Felicity? Miss Hamilton?'

His knock meeting with no response, he had pushed open the door and come into the room, dark eyes going immediately to her wan, pale face.

'What is it?' he asked sharply and, beyond pretence, incapable of holding back she had lifted her hands to gesture towards the ornate headdress, clenching her fingers in a gesture of impatient despondency.

'It's this...' she wailed. 'This damn veil! I can't get it off. I think I'm locked into it for ever!'

She had fully expected him to laugh, or make some impatient masculine comment about the foolishness of being persuaded by female vanity into such a tortuous arrangement. He did neither. Instead he soothed her fractious mood with easy words, reassured her softly, and set to work on the headdress at once, removing the fine hairpins with swift efficiency.

And he had been so unbelievably gentle. Where she had tugged and pulled at her own hair, bringing tears of pain to her eyes and only succeeding in making matters worse, he had seemed to have the magical touch. The pins almost melted away. Within seconds, the veil was freed and tossed aside, the tiara eased from her head and placed carefully on the dressing table.

But he hadn't stopped there.

'You're appallingly tense,' he had murmured, long fingers testing the muscles at the back of her neck, feeling how tight they were.

'And does that surprise you?' Felicity flung at him, grey eyes dark with reproach. 'I mean, I'm having such a *wonderful* time! This should have been my wedding night, instead of which I'm God knows where, with a man who—who...'

Her voice cracked, died painfully, as her control shattered completely and tears welled up in her eyes, shimmering in the evening light.

'What—what are you going to do to me?'

'Nothing.'

Rico's tone was low and emphatic, tight with conviction,

and he reached out and captured her face in both his hands, hard palms lying warm against the softness of her cheeks.

'*Nothing!* I swear to you, *gatita*, that you will come to no harm. My quarrel is not with you, but with the man you were supposed to marry. All I need from you is that you stay here until certain things are sorted out.'

'What sort of things?'

It was disturbing how much she wanted to believe him—shocking to realise that she was already halfway to doing that. That appealingly accented voice held the ring of total conviction, and the black coffee eyes burned into hers as if willing her to accept that he spoke nothing but the truth.

'What has to be sorted out?'

But it was obvious that he wasn't going to answer that. Rejection of her question was stamped into every line of his face, cooling the fires in those dark eyes, changing his expression swiftly and dramatically.

'It isn't necessary for you to know that,' he answered with a curtness that made her flinch inwardly. 'That is my business and none of yours. All you need to know is that you are quite safe. In fact, if you are sensible and do as you are told, and don't do anything foolish like trying to escape in the night, you might find that your captivity here will last no more than a day.'

Right now, even that seemed like an eternity. But it seemed it was the only concession Rico was prepared to offer.

'I'll think about it,' she managed, unwilling in her turn to give too much away.

'Do that,' he murmured, his voice gentling again. 'Do that, *mi belleza* Felicity, and perhaps we will be able—if not to make peace, then at least to come to some sort of understanding we can both live with.'

And as he spoke his hands moved again, sliding into the loosened tangles of her hair, smoothing through the tousled blonde strands, gently combing the knots out of them. Strong fingers kneaded her scalp, finding and easing the tightness of muscle that was like a band of steel around her head, massaging it away until she sighed with weary relief.

'Coffee.'

Felicity started out of her recollections as Rico placed a mug of steaming coffee on the table in front of her.

'Thanks.'

It was just a vague murmur as she struggled to force her mind to concentrate on the present. That had been her mistake earlier. Weakly and foolishly she had let the memory of how gentle Rico could be distract her. She had let her guard down for one vulnerable moment, and he had taken full advantage of the fact.

'What would you like to eat? I was going to offer you breakfast, but perhaps that should really be brunch.'

'Anything. I'm not really all that hungry.'

She looked like a small, stray kitten sitting there, hunched up in her chair in the oversized shirt and jeans, Rico thought, wincing as his conscience gave a painful twist of reproach. With her beautiful skin clear of any sort of make-up, and the fine blonde hair hanging loose about her face, she was just a shadow of the woman she had been yesterday—the woman who had given as good as she got and had fought him every inch of the way.

Except for that one moment last night when she had let her guard down.

'Infierno!'

He cursed under his breath as his conscience tormented him again. *That* Felicity Hamilton had had him seriously doubting the truth of his half-sister's story. If he hadn't made promises he couldn't break, he would have put her in the car right there and then and driven her straight back home to her family. And yet...

Frowning, he stirred his coffee with unnecessary force.

She had shown precious little concern about the fiancé she had left waiting at the altar. And within less than twenty-four hours she had been in his bed—unfaithful to the man she had been about to marry. There were two very distinct sides to Felicity Hamilton and he didn't know which one to trust.

If only he had been able to get through to Maria he might have been able to clear up some of this confusion. But each time he phoned he was informed that the mobile he was calling was switched off.

'You'll wear a hole in the bottom of that mug if you stir that coffee any more.'

The faint touch of humour was the last thing he had expected, and the small smile on the soft mouth, a hint of light in the slightly bruised looking eyes disturbed his already uneasy conscience again, pushing him into action.

'Here…'

Felicity blinked in confusion at the mobile phone he dumped on the table in front of her.

'What…?'

'Ring your father,' Rico commanded brusquely. 'Find out what's happening.'

'Ring…'

She couldn't believe what she was hearing. Was he really going to let her go, just like that? Oh, she knew he'd promised but she'd never truly believed him.

'If the news is good then you'll be on your way home.'

'What exactly is good news?'

His shrug was swift, dismissive.

'You tell me what your father says and I'll tell you if it's good.'

'Fine.'

She struggled for a lightness she was far from feeling. It was his indifference, the total blankness of his eyes and

face that stung most. Did he truly care so little about the
fact that she might be leaving?

Oh, face facts, Fliss! she reproved herself sharply. What
else had she expected? She knew what this man was, an
opportunist and a brigand. He had had all he wanted from
her and now he wanted rid of her. But she was dammed if
she'd let him see even for a second just what that did to
her.

'Okay, then, I'll hope for good news.' She stunned herself by even managing a smile, though it was one that was
very definitely frayed at the edges. 'For both our sakes.'

That smile twisted sharply in Rico's nerves. Did she have
to look so damned pleased—so keen to be gone? But then
what had he expected? That she would beg him to let her
stay?

'Dad? It's me—Fliss. What? … Oh, yes, I'm fine. How
are things with you?… *What?…*'

She struggled to hear her father's words through the roaring in her head, unable to believe what she was hearing.
Her stunned grey eyes flew to Rico's intently watchful face,
clashing sharply with his coldly assessing stare.

Did he know about this? What did this news mean for
her own situation? And, most importantly, would Rico consider it good or bad?

Somehow she managed to bring the conversation to a
halt, promising to ring again as soon as possible. When she
had switched off the phone she simply sat, staring unseeingly at the opposite wall, a thousand disjointed thoughts
whirling inside her head.

'Well?'

Rico pounced as soon as she had switched the phone off.

'I don't understand. Dad says Edward's disappeared—
that he's run off with someone else—some other woman.'

It didn't sound any more credible once she'd said it out
loud. And she couldn't even begin to tell whether Rico

regarded it as good news or the opposite. His face was giving nothing away and the dark stream of Spanish with which he greeted the news was totally incomprehensible to her.

'What? Rico, don't do this to me!' she protested. 'You know I don't understand Spanish. What are you saying?'

But he simply ignored her question, focussing only on the one thing that was important to him.

'This woman...'

Coming to the chair in which she was sitting, he rested one bronzed hand on the back of it, the other on the table at her side, effectively imprisoning her in her place.

'Did she have a name? Did your father say who she was?'

Why did it matter so much to him? Because it did matter. That much was obvious from the burn of something dangerous in the darkness of his eyes.

'Y-yes. Yes, he did. It's Llewellyn. Her name's Maria Llewellyn.'

What she couldn't tell him was that she had heard that name before—and where.

But Rico didn't seem to need any input from her. Instead, his face was filled with a dark satisfaction and he gave a sharp nod of approval of her words.

'*Bueno!*' he said, easing from his position hemming her in. 'Just what I wanted.'

Her thoughts still completely unfocussed, Felicity could watch him in silence.

Just what he wanted? She was lost. What *had* he wanted? She had thought that all his anger was directed against Edward. That it was Edward he wanted to suffer in all this. But now it seemed that what gave him satisfaction was the news that Edward had someone new in his life. And that someone was the only person Felicity had ever heard her former fiancé ever speak of with true warmth. The woman he had once admitted had stolen his heart.

So did Rico actually want Edward to be *happy*?

And if that was the case, what were the possible repercussions for herself and her father?

'This—this is the *good* news?' she managed, unable to believe that could be true.

But Rico nodded firmly, even allowing himself a small, grim smile of gratification.

'The best.'

'But...'

She felt as if her world had been turned upside down and inside out. If it wasn't Edward that Rico had been after all this time, then who was his intended victim?

Had it after all been so much more personal than she had realised? Had he really been after *her* right from the start?

'I don't understand.'

The look Rico slanted in her direction did nothing to ease her whirling thoughts, the panic that was growing by the second, threatening to swamp her completely.

'You don't have to understand, *gatita*. You can leave that to me. All you need to know is that this is good news for you too. Your imprisonment is over. You can go home today.'

CHAPTER NINE

''You can go home today.'

Just like that.

Was it possible? Or was he just cruelly playing with her emotions as a cat might toy with a mouse before finally delivering the deathblow?

'Do you mean that?'

'Mean it?'

Rico looked stunned that she had even had the temerity to ask.

'Of course I mean it. Why would I say it if I meant something else?'

It still didn't seem real. She couldn't imagine why, having gone to the trouble of capturing her, keeping her here, he was going to let her go so easily and so quickly.

Rico had turned away to the worktop and was pulling open a drawer, taking out knives and forks.

'You can leave as soon as you like. You'd better eat something first; then you can go home.'

Go home.

Last night that statement would have sounded like the most wonderful words in all the world, but somehow today they felt like the last straw. It was like being slapped hard in the face when she was already down so that she didn't know what to think.

She only knew that memory after memory was piling up inside her head, destroying any pleasure she might take in the prospect of going home and making her feel desolate and despairing.

Go home to what? To the mess that her father had created of his life and see him arrested for embezzlement? To watch her mother, already weak and ill, grow worse as a result of the shock?

And what about herself? What did the future hold for her? No Edward, no marriage—no Rico.

Hot bitter tears welled in her eyes, blurring her vision, and she couldn't bear the thought that Rico might see them. Pushing back her chair with an ugly scraping sound on the floor, she got clumsily to her feet and headed for the door.

'Felicity!'

Rico's voice was sharp and reproving.

'Where do you think you're going?'

'To get ready,' Felicity muttered, keeping her head stubbornly averted. 'You said I could go.'

Yes, he'd said she could go—but did she have to make it quite so plain that she couldn't wait to get out of here? That she was desperate to turn her back and leave?

But what else had he expected? He'd be every kind of a fool to believe that her behaviour was motivated by anything other than just a physical passion that had taken her as much by surprise as it had him. He'd been stunned by the way he'd wanted her—still wanted her, his body tightening simply at the memory of the hours they had spent in bed—but lust was all it was. How could there be anything more in a relationship with a woman who had been going to marry one man at the start of the day and had ended up in another's bed less than twenty-four hours later?

And yet somehow he couldn't just watch her walk out on him like this.

'You can't...'

Madre de Dios, what was wrong with him? Was he actually going to plead with her to stay? Hastily he readjusted his tone.

'You haven't eaten.'

'I'm not hungry.'

Food would choke her. She would never get it past the hard, solid knot that had formed in her throat, closing it off. And if she stayed then Rico would be sure to spot the betraying sheen of tears in her eyes and know her pretence of carelessness for the act it was.

And she couldn't bear that.

'But you haven't had anything since last night. You'll make yourself ill. What about some—?'

'I told you, I'm not hungry!'

It was a wail of panic, of fear that he might stop her, force her back into the room. She was almost at the door. But her tear-hazed eyes were too blurred to see clearly and she blundered clumsily into the large pine dresser that stood against the wall, biting her lip hard to hold back the cry of pain that almost escaped her.

'Felicity!' Her name was a sound of pure exasperation as if it came through gritted teeth. 'Sit down!'

Stubbornly she shook her head.

'I said, sit down!'

'And I said I don't want anything to eat.'

'*Por Dios*, woman, will you do as you are told!'

He was definitely losing his already shaky grip on his temper now.

'No, I will not!'

Oh, why wouldn't this door open? Perhaps the fact that she could hardly see it had something to do with it, but she had turned and turned the handle and all to no avail.

'Felicity…' It was a warning, low-voiced and dangerous, but one she was determined to ignore.

'Stop ordering me around!'

'And you stop arguing with me over everything. You're only making things so much harder for yourself. Felicity…'

Strong hands closed over her arm, stilling her frantic movements, and swung her round to face him.

'Be sensible! This is not getting you anywhere.'

'I—I don't feel sensible.'

To her horror her voice quavered revealingly on the word.

'I feel—I feel...'

Just when she was least able to handle it, she heard a sudden vivid echo of her father's voice at the other end of the phone line when she had spoken to him earlier.

'Edward's run off with some other woman—he left a message saying he loved her, that he planned to marry this Maria, that your wedding was off. But now that Ricardo Valeron's in the picture, none of that matters any more, does it, sweetie? Now that you and he are together we're quite all right. We're more than all right...'

Suddenly, shockingly, things just would not be held back. The tears she had fought against so fiercely overwhelmed her, spilling from her eyes and cascading down her cheeks.

'Felicity? *Gatita...*?'

The sudden gentling of his voice, the use of that caressing 'gatita', was positively the last straw. Unable to hide her feelings any longer, she buried her face in his shirt, her cheek against the hard wall of his chest, gave herself up to the fear and the unhappiness, and wept.

'What the...? Felicity...?'

Where the hell had this come from? Just what had provoked this storm of weeping?

'*Tears?* Why?'

But she could only shake her head and sob more.

Gently he eased her back into the room, folding his arms round her and holding her. There was no point in any further questions, at least not until the storm had passed.

But he didn't feel at all comfortable. His conscience was uneasy and making him feel angry at the circumstances that had led to this, at Maria for her drama queen behaviour, her demanding of promises. But most of all he felt angry at himself for not reading the situation right.

He had believed Maria when she had declared that Felicity didn't love Edward Venables. His half-sister had claimed that there was no way this marriage was going to be based on love or any real feeling. And he had *believed* her.

And until now, the way that Felicity had behaved had only seemed to add fuel to the fires of contempt he had felt for this woman. She had appeared to be nothing but a cheap slut, slipping from one man's bed into another without a second thought, never pausing for a moment to even think of Venables.

But if that was the case then why this sudden attack of weeping? Could it be a belated conscience, or because of the news she'd just received? Was she truly this upset at the thought that Venables was with someone else? He didn't like the way that made him feel. The uncomfortable sense of guilt combined with something he knew was dangerously close to jealous envy at the thought of this woman actually caring for the other man.

But added to this already volatile mixture, threatening to make it even more potently explosive with every second that ticked by, was the constant burning physical hunger he felt for Felicity. A hunger that gnawed away at his insides, leaving them raw and sensitive, arousing his body and inflaming his mind in the most dangerous way.

Slowly, gradually, Felicity's sobs became less violent, less desperate, until eventually they shuddered to a halt, leaving her breathing rather raggedly, sniffing inelegantly. Reaching across to the box of tissues that stood on the dresser, Rico pulled out a bunch and wiped her tearstained cheeks with a considered gentleness that twisted in her heart.

'So now, *gatita*,' he said softly, his tone almost a caress in itself. 'Can you talk now? Are you prepared to tell me what all this is about? You should feel happy, not sad. I have said you can go home…'

'But that's just it!'

The struggle she had to hide so much of what she was really feeling made her voice higher and sharper than she had ever intended.

'You don't want to go home?'

'Yes, yes, I do—but…'

Despairingly she shook her head.

'But it's not my story to tell.'

'Then whose story is it?'

Keen brown eyes narrowed sharply and she knew that he had guessed even before he spoke.

'It was the phone call that upset you, so this has something to do with Edward.'

She couldn't meet his eyes, knowing her own cloudy grey ones would give away too much. But she knew that he would insist on some response and all she could do was nod slowly, keeping her downbent gaze fixed on the floor.

It *was* something to do with Edward. She didn't dare to tell Rico about the sorry mess that Joe Hamilton had got himself into. She had no idea how much he already knew; she only knew that Edward had promised her he would keep it from the Argentinian if she did as he said.

If her one-time groom had kept his word, then there was still a chance that all might not be lost as far as her father was concerned. It was only a tiny chance, but if there was any hope at all she was going to snatch at it. Not to do so was to risk too much and, with her mother's health still so precarious, she would do anything at all to prevent the truth getting out.

'Yes, it's about Edward,' she whispered unhappily.

It wasn't all of it, but that was more than she was prepared to admit to. Besides, there was so much that she couldn't bring herself to acknowledge, even to herself. She didn't understand half of it so how could she explain any of it to Rico? He was too tangled up in all this for her to be able to think straight about him.

'So tell me.'

He was moving as he spoke, leading her back towards the table. Easing her into a chair, he looked down at the now cold coffees with a grimace of distaste and hurriedly emptied the mugs into the sink. He felt better if he was doing something. At least it kept his hands occupied and distracted his thoughts.

Felicity wished he would look at her. It was so hard to say this to that stiff, straight back. If she could just see his face...

But then Rico swung round and she realised her mistake. Seeing his expression was far worse than she had ever anticipated. The contempt that seared over her skin seemed to burn everywhere it touched, and the tight muscles in the ruthless jaw pulled his beautiful mouth into a hard, uncompromising line.

'What about Edward?'

'He—he needed a wife.'

She had to fight to force the words out.

'His grandfather—Lord Highson—totally disapproved of his lifestyle and had threatened to disinherit him. What he wanted was to see Edward married and settled down. If he—if he found a suitable bride before the end of the year then his grandfather would keep him in his will. He'd get the money, Highson House and the title—and Edward wanted that title.'

But Rico wasn't listening. His mind seemed to have tuned out Edward's part in all this. All he could think of was Felicity and the way that she had been prepared to sell herself...

His face set rigid. He didn't like the way this was heading at all.

'He—he asked me to help him.'

'Why you?'

'I was the sort of bride his grandfather had in mind. The right age, the right background...'

Her mouth twisted bitterly.

'The right sort of breeding stock, I suppose. And Lord Highson very definitely wanted another heir to the dynasty.'

This was nothing more than the complete truth. Edward had been totally blunt about the advantages she could bring to their proposed union. She was everything his grandfather would approve of—and light years away from the one woman Edward Venables had ever truly cared for—the wild, exotic, slightly scandalous Maria Llewellyn.

'And what would you get out of this?'

Felicity swallowed hard but found that her throat still felt knotted and constricted. She had known that this was inevitable. This question had to come, but she was still totally unprepared to answer it. Just what could she say that would sound both convincing and in character?

Except for the truth.

'Money.'

She forced the word out on a hoarse, raw croak, hating the sound of it. It was the truth but only a tiny part of it. The only part she could let Rico know. The rest of it was too problematic, too dangerous, to reveal. Just the thought of the probable consequences if she did made her shudder in horror deep inside.

'Money.' Rico made his repetition of the noun sound like a violent curse. 'I take it you needed a lot of money.'

'Thousands.'

In her mind's eye she was picturing her father's ashen face when he'd told her. The tremor in his voice as he'd pleaded with her not to say anything to her mother for fear of worsening her already bad health.

'And Edward offered to give you what you needed?'

'Yes.'

It was just a thin sliver of sound, one he must have had to strain to hear.

He didn't ask *why* she had needed the money, Felicity noted. He just stood there, strong arms folded tight across the width of his chest, dark eyes cold with contempt, like judge and jury all rolled into one.

'In return for marrying him?'

'Yes.'

'He'd pay off all your debts?'

'Yes.'

'So you didn't love him?'

He was having a hard time getting his head round this, all the more so because at certain points since this morning he'd actually come to start doubting Maria's version of the story. He'd even doubted the reports he'd been given about Felicity. The stories of her long, long nights spent at the same nightclub.

Those damn tears of hers had got to him—the tears and the delicate vulnerability of her beauty had ruined his usually very rational judgement.

Foolishly he'd allowed himself to be swayed by the way she looked, the way she seemed. And because he'd actually started to feel sorry for her, to cast himself as the villain in all this, the kickback of anger and disappointment was all the more bitter now. At his sides his hands clenched over the edge of the worktop against which he was leaning, tightening until the knuckles showed white as he struggled to rein in his dangerously savage temper.

'You didn't love him?' he barked coldly, deriving some satisfaction from the way that the sound of his voice brought her head up sharply, smoke grey eyes widening in shock.

'No I didn't love him. It—it was just a marriage of convenience.'

'Very convenient.'

His sneering tone and the look of censure he subjected her to was positively the last straw.

'Of course you wouldn't understand that!' she flung at him, defiance laced with bitterness burning on her tongue.

'I have to admit that I don't,' was the swift reply, the lazily indifferent drawl hiding a cool condemnation that caught her on the raw like the stinging flick of a whip.

'No, you wouldn't know what it's like to need money really desperately—the sort of money you can never possibly afford to repay. More money than you could ever hope to earn in your lifetime! I suppose to you it would be just pocket money! Something you could toss aside without even noticing it.'

'Are you suggesting that *I* should pay off your debts?'

'*No!* Oh, no! That's the last thing I want.'

'Is it?'

Slowly Rico straightened up from where he had been leaning against the marble worktop, his movement indolently controlled. But all the same Felicity flinched inside at the thought of the leashed power of his body, the honed strength of every muscle and sinew, the unyielding hardness of bone that made up his impressive physique. He made her think of some ruthless predator silently prowling through the night, waiting for the perfect moment to spring. She couldn't stay sitting down any longer and pushed herself to her feet as she angrily refuted the accusation.

'Of course it is! It never even crossed my mind!'

'Then perhaps it should have done.'

'*What?*'

Stupefied, she could only stare at him with shock-hazed

eyes, her pupils wide and unfocussed. Had he really said what she thought she had heard? But even if he had, there was a black irony about the situation that made her quail inside. He couldn't pay off her debts—her father's debts— because *he* was the person the money was owed to. He was offering to give her the money to pay himself back, and he didn't even realise it.

'What—what did you say?'

Rico's sensual mouth curled briefly at the corners into the sort of smile that held no warmth but instead sent a sensation of something cold and nastily slimy slithering slowly down the length of her spine.

'I simply suggested that, seeing as your scheme to marry into the aristocracy has come to a grinding halt, then perhaps the next logical step would be for you to find another suitable candidate. Someone else to help you out of your financial difficulties.'

'And you are putting yourself forward as that "suitable candidate"?'

His shrug dismissed the shake of disbelief in her voice in the same moment that his eyes challenged her to test out her theory.

'Would you really?'

It slipped past her unguarded lips before she had a chance to bite it back. Perhaps she had him all wrong. Perhaps he really did want to help.

Her heart gave a sudden, unexpected little skip of hope. Was it possible that Rico too had experienced something of the same sort of tug of attraction that she felt towards him? Perhaps if she told him the truth they could work something out.

'You'd do that for me?'

This time his smile was all cruelty, fiendish and malign.

'For a price.'

'Oh!'

All her new-found hope fled like air escaping from a pricked balloon, destroyed before it had fully formed. All she was left with was a terrible sense of disillusionment and desolation, the feeling all the more devastating because of the momentary experience of hope she had allowed herself to feel just a moment before.

'And I suppose I don't have to ask what that price would be?'

It was there, in the darkness of his eyes, the intensity of his gaze. It was stamped into the sensual appreciation that showed on his face, written so clearly that she could almost see the words burning between them in letters of fire.

The price of her salvation was her, in this man's bed, for as long as he chose.

'You want me to—to sleep with you. You want to buy my body for your use!'

He didn't even make a pretence at denying it, though he shrugged off her indignant fury with another casual lift of those powerful shoulders under the navy shirt.

'I want more of what we shared this morning,' he stated bluntly, ebony eyes locking with furious grey. 'I'm not ashamed to admit that. I enjoyed—hell, I more than enjoyed it! I've never known anything like it in my life, and I'd pay any price to experience that again.'

I'd pay any price—he really knew how to hurt. The words stabbed straight to her heart, slashing into the vulnerable core of her. All he was offering her was a sexual affair. All he wanted from her was more sex, more passion—with no emotion thrown in. And he thought that *he* was the one paying a price for it.

With an effort that cost her more than she dared admit to, she forced herself to draw herself up, face that coldly challenging expression with at least a pretence at calm when deep down she was dying inside.

'Well, you can you can relax, Señor I-Want-More

Valeron. More importantly, you can keep your precious cash in whatever Swiss bank account you've hidden it. I wouldn't touch it if I was desperate.'

'But you are desperate,' Rico reminded her brutally.

'Not *that* desperate!' Felicity flung back at him, her throat aching with all she was keeping back. 'I wouldn't touch your money to save my life! I don't want anything from you—anything at all!'

'You're a liar,' he returned with deadly softness. 'You want this every bit as much as I do.'

'No, I don't!'

If she said it often enough, loudly enough, she might actually convince him. She would never convince herself; she'd accepted that already. No matter how many times she said she didn't want him, her poor, weak, foolish heart would never accept it as the truth.

'I don't want you—I don't want your money—I don't want anything from you, ever!'

'But you were prepared to take what Venables offered. You didn't think twice, then—practically snatched his hand off without thinking. I can give you more than he ever could…'

He really believed she could do it. He really thought that she could just substitute one rich man for another without a tinge of conscience. Felicity's stomach heaved nauseously and she had to reach out a shaking hand to rest on the nearest chair for support to hold herself upright.

'Financially, perhaps! But that's all!'

She felt as if she was fighting for her life; as if, emotionally at least, she had been driven into a dangerous corner, with her back well and truly up against the wall.

'Edward was prepared to give me more than that.'

'Oh, sure!' Rico scorned. 'In what way?'

'He offered me marriage! That's what makes the difference! He didn't just suggest I occupied his bed for the night, became his—his mistress—his sex toy! He offered me a ring and his name—I take it that doesn't come with the deal you're suggesting?'

She knew his answer before he spoke. It was there in the sudden change in his face, the bleakness of his eyes, the clamping tight of the beautiful mouth into a thin, harsh line of rejection of even the thought.

'No way,' he muttered roughly. 'I have more pride—'

'And so do I!'

Somehow she managed to lift her chin proudly, stare him straight in the eye, deliberately blanking out her thoughts so that he wouldn't be able to tell how she was bleeding to death inside.

'I have more pride than to accept the second-rate deal you suggest. The price tag attached to it is way too high. If you offered me all the money you possessed and I had to take you too, then it would still come far too expensive! I'd rather go back to working all day and all night to pay off my fa—my debts bit by bit, even if it takes me the rest of my life!'

Which it probably would, she acknowledged miserably. She would have to go home and tell her father that she hadn't been able to save him. She would have to be there for her mother when Claire Hamilton found out the truth about her husband's behaviour. But she had no alternative. Anything, even that, was better than becoming this man's sex slave.

'*Esta bien!*' Rico's response was clipped, curt, icy cold. 'I will not ask again.'

'I won't give you the chance!' Felicity declared fervently. 'Because after today if I never, ever see you again it will be just the way I want things.'

Her betrayed heart cried out in anguished protest at the damage her lie had inflicted on it but she forced herself to ignore it, once more hiding behind the mask of control that she had used so often she was actually beginning to feel accustomed to it.

'And now, if you don't mind, I'd appreciate it if you kept your word and let me leave.'

The mask wavered just for a second, threatened to slip, when he actually hesitated and it looked for a moment as if he might be about to retract his agreement to her leaving.

'I can go home?' she questioned shakily, only relaxing when he inclined his dark head in agreement.

'Of course. I'll fetch the car. We can leave at once.'

And if she had needed any more evidence as to just how little her feelings, her response to his suggestion, had meant to him it was there in the ease with which he accepted her decision, the speed with which he prepared to take her home.

He didn't even feel she was worth arguing with, and he had dismissed her from his thoughts in the space of a heartbeat.

And the pain that casual cruelty caused brought home to Felicity the appalling truth that things would never be that way for her. She would never be able to switch off from Rico as he had done from her. In fact, she doubted that she would ever be able to forget him for the rest of her life, and with that doubt came a warning that the pain she was feeling now was really only the beginning.

CHAPTER TEN

'IT'S on the right, here...'

As Rico manoeuvred the car into the centre of the road and then round the corner she had indicated, Felicity sank back into her seat with a sigh of intense relief and closed her eyes in the first real moment of relaxation she had known for almost thirty-six hours.

They were here. They had reached the street where she lived and the nightmare her life had become was almost all over. In another couple of minutes, Rico would park outside the large old Victorian house on the first floor of which she had a tiny, one-bedroomed flat, and she would be able to get out and walk away.

She was determined she would do so without a backward glance, no matter what it would cost her. She wouldn't give him so much as a hint of the way he had hurt her, the misery that was eating her up inside. She would say good-bye, keeping her tone as casual as possible, perhaps even manage an airy wave, and then she would walk firmly into the house and close the door on him.

What would happen after that, the way she might react once the defence of the solid wooden door was in place, she didn't know. She didn't even want to consider it now; it would weaken her too much. The time would come soon enough, and then...

'What the...?'

Rico's harsh exclamation, the faint screech of the brakes as he performed an abrupt emergency stop, had her eyes flying open in shock to stare at him in dazed bemusement.

'What is it? What's wrong? Is there...'

The words died on her tongue as Rico's silent nod of his dark head drew her attention forward and through the windscreen to where a large crowd had gathered on the doorstep of one of the properties halfway down the road. There were perhaps twenty-five or more men and women, all just standing about, chatting desultorily, making her frown in confused bewilderment.

'Who—what are they doing?'

But even as she spoke things came more into focus and realisation dawned like a blow to her head.

The crowd wasn't just gathered there for some casual meeting. They were there for a purpose—and that purpose was clear from the cameras and microphones they held, the vans parked on each side of the street, the names of television and radio stations emblazoned on their sides. And they weren't outside just any house in the street, but one in particular—the house where she lived.

'They're reporters!' she gasped. 'Something must have happened...'

'*You've* happened,' Rico returned with cynical emphasis. 'You and the wedding of the year—the wedding that never was.'

He slammed his fist hard against the steering wheel in a gesture of angry frustration.

'I should have seen this coming. I should have known!'

'No, that can't...' Felicity began but she couldn't complete the sentence because even as she spoke there was a change in the group outside her house.

Someone looked up, their attention caught by the way the car had stopped and was still stationary in the middle of the road, not going anywhere, but not parking either.

'They've noticed us.' Rico spoke sharply, the edge to his voice communicating a mood that made her tense sharply, nerves twisting tight as she sat upright in her seat. 'They're coming.'

And the bunch of people was in fact in motion, all of them heading their way. Through the open window Felicity could already hear the buzz of intrigued, excited conversation and it made her skin prickle with unease.

'You're going to have to make a decision. Do we stay or do we go?'

'Go where? There is nowhere else to go.'

When she'd told Rico to bring her here, to her flat, it had been because she couldn't think of anywhere else. If she went to her parents' house she would have to face their concern, their questions, her father's fears about his future—and she wasn't ready for that. She needed a little time on her own; time to draw breath and collect her thoughts, before she could face anyone again.

'That's your choice. But if you don't make it fast we won't be able to get out of here.'

'But I don't want to go anywhere! I want to go home.'

'Right—that's your decision. But don't expect this to be pleasant.'

He edged the car to the side of the road where already the reporters were gathering, swarming round the vehicle, brandishing microphones and cameras. Felicity flinched back in her seat, crying out in shock as the flash of a dozen or so bulbs exploded right in her face it seemed, blinding her momentarily.

'What is it? What's going on?'

She had her hand on the door as she spoke, but before she could open it, Rico caught her arm, holding her back.

'One word of advice,' he said sharply. 'Don't say a word—not even ''no comment''. Just keep your mouth shut, your head down, and walk straight through them. It'll be easier for you that way.'

'Easier? But you must have it wrong. They can't have come to see *me*! I mean, why would they? What…?'

But even as she spoke the sounds from outside reached

her. Loud and assertive, and determined to be heard. And every single person was calling her name.

'Felicity...'

'Miss Hamilton...'

'Just a minute of your time, Felicity...'

'Just a couple of questions...'

Panic clutched at her throat, her heart pounding fearfully, and she turned to Rico with wide, stunned eyes.

'I can't! I can't go out there.'

'You have to,' he told her firmly. 'It's too late to turn back now. If you want to get to your flat you're going to have to go through them. It's that or get out of here fast.'

If she wanted to get to her flat! To Felicity, who could just see the window of her sitting room through the press of people round the car, the thought of her small, shabby apartment seemed like some peaceful haven, a refuge from the storm that had so suddenly and unexpectedly erupted around her. She had never wanted to be anywhere so much in all her life.

'Don't worry...'

Once again Rico seemed to have picked up on her thoughts.

'I'll be right behind you and I'll stay with you every step of the way.'

That wasn't exactly how she'd planned that things would be. The idea of Rico coming with her, of him coming into her flat, into her home, shook what little was left of Felicity's composure. It was disturbing, uncomfortable, un-wanted—but at the same time so comforting that she knew she couldn't refuse it.

Drawing in a deep, calming breath, she straightened her shoulders and swallowed hard.

'Let's get this over with...' she muttered and pushed open the door.

It was like stepping out into the eye of a storm. All

around her there was noise, the whirr of camera shutters, the pop of flash bulbs, the shuffle of footsteps on the pavement. And all the time there was the sound of her name—'Felicity…Felicity…Felicity…' Over and over and over again, mixed with the constant cries of, 'Just one question…'

She was pushed and harassed, jostled and bruised, microphones were shoved right into her face so that she had to jerk her head backwards for fear they might actually bang into her mouth.

'Why did you do it, Felicity? Did you have second thoughts? Wedding day nerves?'

'Did you ever love him really? Or were you just…?'

'When did you meet Ricardo Valeron? Where…?'

She couldn't do this! Panic froze her feet to the ground, blinded her eyes, so that she couldn't move or see a way through. She didn't even know which direction led to her flat, couldn't have made it there if she tried. She felt as if she was drowning in a sea of bodies and questions and very definitely going down for the third time.

'Rico!'

It was a wail of panic, high-pitched and tight, but it was swallowed up in the furore surrounding her, lost in the waves of noise that swirled round her head.

But then, just as she was about to lose control completely, suddenly Rico was there at her side, tall and strong and solidly dependable. A source of support and calm in a world gone mad.

One arm came round her shoulders, heavy and warm, drawing her close to him so that her cheek was against his chest, her face protected from the cameras and microphones by the shielding fingers of one powerful hand. Instinctively her hands went round his waist, clutching at his jacket for support.

'Just walk…' he said calmly in her ear, the warmth of

his breath caressing her skin. 'Just put one foot in front of the other and don't stop. I'll make sure you're going the right way.'

She could do nothing but obey him. Incapable of thinking for herself she let him half walk, half carry her on to the pavement and slowly, gradually, through the crowd.

And now the cameras were turned in his direction, the questions directed at him.

'Where did you two meet, Ricardo?'

'Is this true love or just another take-over deal?'

'When can we expect to hear an announcement? A wedding date?'

But if they expected any answers, they were disappointed. Rico neither said a word nor reacted in any way. Instead he just kept on walking steadily and easily, pushing his way through the crowd, heading directly for the house.

There was a moment of uncomfortable hesitation when, at the top of the small flight of steps, he paused and turned to Felicity.

'Key?'

A sense of despair swept through Felicity, threatening to take her legs from under her. Of course, her keys were with her mother, in the handbag she had been expecting to collect after the ceremony, when she changed out of her wedding dress and into her going away outfit.

'I don't…' she began, but Rico had already acted.

Noticing what she had missed, the way that the door was in fact not fully closed but that some other tenant, on their way out, had simply let it swing to and the latch hadn't caught, he nudged it open with one elegantly booted foot, swinging her inside with him. Even as they made it indoors, he had turned and slammed the door closed again, right in the faces of the pursuing reporters.

'That should hold them for a while,' he muttered in grim

satisfaction. 'At least long enough to give you a breathing space. Now—which flat?'

'Upstairs—the first door on the right,' Felicity managed, drawing in a deep, uneven breath as she felt some of the tension slip away from her with the realisation that she was safe.

'I can manage by myself,' she added as Rico offered her his arm again.

The help she had been only too glad to receive outside seemed to have taken on a whole new image in the house and behind closed doors. Somehow, what had seemed only protective and supportive there now felt much more intimate and personal, far harder to accept. It sparked off totally different feelings inside her, making her blood warm in her veins, her heartbeat accelerate dangerously, and sent her hurrying up the stairs with her skin tingling alarmingly.

And Rico was still there, just behind her, keeping his distance but at the same time making it plain that if she needed him he was there, ready to help. It seemed he felt the change too because he didn't touch her at all but held back, coming to a careful halt several feet away from her, his long body held stiff and taut, preserving the distance between them.

'At least I do have a key for this door...'

She tried for laughter but felt it fade as he watched her take her key from its hiding place on top of the door frame, his frown revealing only too clearly his disapproval of such a casual disregard for security.

'Not exactly sensible,' was his dry comment, his tone catching Felicity on the raw.

'I don't care if you think it's sensible!' she tossed back at him. 'Everyone else in this house is a friend—I trust them. Besides, it's not as if there's anything anyone would want to steal in here...'

She was struggling to appear relaxed but found herself

failing miserably when the hand that held the key shook so much in the aftermath of her ordeal outside that she found it impossible to push it into the lock. Rico was itching to move forward and take it from her in order to do the job himself, she knew, but she repelled him with a glare, managing it on the second attempt, and throwing the door open on a slightly wild gesture.

'See!' she announced, indicating the small green and cream painted sitting room with a wave of her hand. 'Hardly Highson House, is it?'

No, that had been a mistake—a bad one. It had reminded Rico of the reason why she had said she was marrying Edward, putting the frown back on his face, and the distance into his eyes.

'But I love it,' she added with hasty defensiveness. 'It may be a bit run-down and hardly luxurious, but it's home. Come in quickly before that howling pack of hyenas outside finds their way in here.'

'I think we're safe enough for a while,' Rico replied, though he followed her into the room so that she could close the door firmly behind them. 'They're unlikely to follow us in here. But it'll be a different story when you need to go out again.'

Felicity shuddered at just the thought.

'But surely they'll give up before then? They'll get tired of waiting…'

She let the sentence trail off as Rico strode over to the window, holding the curtain back with one bronzed hand as he looked down into the street below.

'Does it look as if this lot is ready to give up?' he enquired sardonically. 'It looks more as if they're planning to stay the night.'

Coming to his side, Felicity peered out too, fear clenching in her stomach as she saw the reporters, still gathered in a pack like the hunting dogs she had compared them to, on and around the doorstep. Some small movement she made must have caught someone's eye because even as she stood there, all the heads lifted as one and turned towards her. Cameras swung in her direction; flash bulbs exploded, sending her reeling back into the centre of the room, and all her hard-won composure vanished in a second.

'Why are they hounding me like this?' she cried. 'What do they think I've done?'

'You've given them a story.' was Rico's response. 'As far as they're concerned they're only doing their job.'

As he spoke he was pulling something from his jacket pocket. He tossed it towards her and she caught it clumsily. It was a sheet from one of the tabloid newspapers, folded up small.

With shaking hands she opened it, smoothed it out, a cry of shock and disbelief escaping her as she saw the headline.

'SECRETARY DITCHES EARL'S HEIR AT THE ALTAR—Felicity does the dishonourable on the Honourable and runs off with Argentine millionaire.'

'Where did you get this?'

'It was on sale at all the motorway services we passed. I bought a copy the time we stopped for coffee.'

When she had been so determined to get back home as quickly as possible that she had only allowed herself the time to gulp down her drink and make a hasty trip to the Ladies, Felicity recalled. She hadn't even spared the newspapers a single glance.

But I didn't "*run off*" with you! They...'

Words failed her as she glanced down at the paper once again.

Beneath the banner headline was a photograph of Edward, elegant in his wedding finery, looking mournful and unhappy with the caption 'broken-hearted'.

'No!'

Her legs giving way beneath her, Felicity sank into the nearest chair, still struggling to take it all in.

'It can't be—Edward wouldn't say that.'

But as she read on she discovered that Edward not only *would* say it, he had. In the report of the 'wedding of the year that never was' she was being billed as a callous heartbreaker, a shallow flirt with an eye to the main chance who had dangled one man on a string, promising to marry him, only to discard him when another, richer prize came along.

'That's not how it happened! They can't print this!'

'They already have done.'

'But it's not true! Not a single word of it.'

'No? Correct me if I'm wrong, but I thought you told me that you were marrying Edward for his money—at least for the money he promised you to pay off your debts.'

His goading incensed her, adding fuel to the fires of emotion that were already burning deep inside her.

'This is all your fault!' she cried indignantly, screwing the paper into a tight ball and throwing it straight into his impassive face. 'You started this! If it wasn't for you and your mad kidnapping scheme, Edward and I would have been married by now and I wouldn't have had to go through any of this, seeing my name dragged through the dirt.'

'And that matters—more than the fact that you didn't get a rich husband to pay off your debts?'

'Of course it matters! How do you think my parents feel, seeing my name plastered all over the papers like this?'

Except of course that her father believed that the fictitious relationship with Rico was an actual fact.

Felicity groaned and buried her face in her hands in a gesture of despair.

'Why is this happening to me? All I want is my life back.'

'I doubt if you'll get that wish for a while.'

Rico was back at the window, standing well away from the glass so that he could observe but not be seen.

'It looks like the word of your whereabouts has already spread. There are reinforcements arriving every minute.'

Felicity turned pale at the thought.

'I can't face them, I just can't. Rico—what am I going to do?'

He wouldn't be human if her appeal didn't affect him, Rico reflected inwardly. When she looked at him like that, with her grey eyes dark with distress against the pallor of her cheeks, it tugged at something sharply in his heart. It made him want to forget all he had learned about her earlier, the disillusionment that had set in when he had learned the true reason behind her planned marriage to Edward Venables.

When they had set out from his house earlier that afternoon his plan had been to bring her here, take her home—and leave her. He wanted nothing more to do with her, wanted out of this situation fast. He couldn't be more aware of the way that his intensely physical response to this woman had clouded his thoughts, distorting his thinking, and pushing him into foolish, potentially dangerous action.

But that was just lust—just his body's hunger talking—and lust didn't last. Sooner or later the fires of desire burned themselves out and all you were left with were the rapidly cooling ashes of what had once been a passionate relationship. He'd been there before, and no doubt he'd be there again. But when he did he'd make sure it was with someone very different from this cold-blooded schemer who saw pound signs whenever she looked at men.

But even as the thoughts formed in his mind he knew they were failing to convince him.

'You can wait it out,' he managed gruffly, refusing to meet the entreaty in her eyes. 'They'll get tired eventually.'

'But how long is eventually? A day? A week?'

She glanced towards the window again and the flash of apprehension in her eyes twisted his conscience uncomfortably.

She looked like a little girl curled up in the big green armchair, her legs tucked underneath her, the oversized shirt and jeans swamping her slender body. But he'd been caught that way once before and had regretted it ever since. The impression of vulnerability and defencelessness was nothing but a façade, a mask behind which she hid her true, grasping nature. He wasn't going to put his head in the noose she dangled a second time.

He just wished his mind could convince his body and not keep reminding him of how it had felt to hold her close, feel the soft velvet of her flesh under his, cup the warm weight of her breasts in his caressing hands. Merely to think of it made his heart pound, drying his mouth in the heat of his memories.

'If you're lucky this whole thing will just be a nine-day wonder.'

The fight he had to make his voice even and indifferent made it harsher than he had anticipated, and he watched her wince sharply as she heard it.

'The minute some new story comes along, they'll drop you like a stone and move on to more interesting ground.'

He was going to leave her, Felicity realised miserably. He was going to abandon her and walk away without a backward look. Less than thirty-six hours ago, that had been exactly what she had wanted. She had prayed to have him out of her life and to be left alone.

Now the prospect of it tore her at heart and left it bleeding.

'Oh, wonderful!' she managed, her voice husky with pain. 'Brilliant! And what do I do in the meantime? Stay locked in here or throw myself to the wolves if I try to go out—*Rico*!'

She broke off on a cry of fear as down below someone started banging on the front door with a heavy fist, the sound reverberating loudly through the hall and up the stair-well.

He couldn't stop himself.

That cry called to everything that was right and moral in his make-up. It appealed to his innate sense of fairness, the primitive instinct of a male, the need to protect and defend his mate when danger threatened.

Before he even had time to think he had moved to her side, coming down onto the side of the chair to gather her close in his arms and hold her tight. She felt so delicate in his grasp, the fine bones almost too fragile to bear his grip.

'Oh, why won't they go away?' Felicity moaned. 'Why won't they leave me alone?'

Once, as a boy, he had rescued a terrified sparrow from the jaws of a predatory cat and carried it carefully to safety. It had trembled in his hands as Felicity did now and he had wondered just how such a frail creature could ever cope with the rigours of the world, the force that nature could throw at it.

It wouldn't survive, his mother had told him. He would have done better to leave it with the cat. Then at least its end would have been mercifully quick. But he wouldn't give in. Something about the small creature had roused every protective instinct he possessed and he had cared for it devotedly, keeping it in a box in his room, feeding it seeds and grubs, until at last it regained its strength. He had never forgotten the moment he had set it free, the way his heart had seemed to soar along with the bird as it spread its wings and flew away.

And something of the same feeling assailed him now. He knew that the only wise, the only *sane* decision to make was to walk away. To tell himself that Felicity had made her own choices, created her own bed. All he had to do was to leave her to lie in it. He should walk through that door, shutting it firmly behind him, and never see her again.

But his conscience wouldn't let him do that.

No, if he was honest, he didn't *want* to do that.

Face facts, you fool! he berated himself inwardly. She's got her hooks into you and you don't want her to let go.

And when the bang at the door came again and Felicity, shivering, reached out and took his hand, folding her fingers round it as if to absorb his strength by doing so, he knew he was lost. His mouth had opened before he had time to think.

'There is one other thing you can do...' he heard himself saying. 'You can always come away with me. After all, it's only what everyone already expects you to do. Come to Argentina until all the fuss dies down.'

CHAPTER ELEVEN

WHAT am I doing here?

It was the question that Felicity had asked herself a dozen or more times ever since the moment Rico's private jet had first landed at the International Airport in Ezeiza, outside Buenos Aires. From there they had transferred to a large helicopter for the flight inland to the huge *estancia* set on the lush green plains of the Pampas that had been the Valeron family home for almost a century.

By then she had already started to wonder just what she was doing, and her first sight of the ranch house at La Estrella had set the question pounding over and over in her head like a nagging refrain.

Why am I here? What on earth possessed me to agree, to accept Rico's invitation?

Because she had never intended to say yes. In fact, even as Rico's words had died away she had already decided that 'no' was the only possible answer. She had actually opened her mouth to say so when another loud bang at the door had broken into her train of thought, stilling the words on her lips.

'They're not going to go away until they get their story,' Rico had said, reading her expression with intuitive astuteness. 'If you stay here they'll only make your life hell, hounding you day and night. Far better to buy yourself a little breathing space by getting out of the country for a while.'

Buy yourself a little breathing space… Common sense and every hope of self-preservation told her that she shouldn't even be considering the idea, but Felicity was stunned to find that she was actually doing more than that. She was looking at the prospect of going with Rico not just in order to gain a little time of peace and quiet, but as a way of buying a little more time *with him*.

It was not much more than twenty-four hours since she had first set eyes on Rico and in that time she had swung from hating and fearing him to passionate, uncontrollable desire for him and back again. Only a very short time ago she had dreamed of getting away from him, of being free of his dangerous, devastating presence in her life and letting herself return to normal. She had wanted nothing more than to see him walk away from her, leaving her to pick up the pieces of her existence.

But now the prospect of a life without Rico in it seemed nothing more than an existence, empty and dull. She couldn't bear to say goodbye; knew that she would do anything, anything at all, if it would only mean that she could stay with him even a short time longer.

It was mad, impossibly crazy, hopelessly irrational, but rational thought didn't come into it. She was listening to her most basic, most primitive instincts and, following their urges, she couldn't even find the control to say yes. Instead she simply nodded, losing the power of speech in the shock of what she was agreeing to.

But that didn't mean she hadn't had second thoughts. The worst moment of doubt had come when the helicopter had started to circle, ready to set down.

Rico had touched her arm to draw her attention and pointed out of the window.

'If you look out now, you will get your first sight of the *estancia*. Over there—see—that is La Estrella.'

'That!'

Felicity's breath caught in her throat and she stared in stunned amazement at the low, spreading house set in the middle of huge lush lawns. It was built in a square around a central courtyard, with white painted walls, a red-tiled roof, and Moorish-looking arched windows opening on to a wide veranda. To one side was the clear water and blue-painted tiles of a large swimming pool, and the enormous garden was planted with banana palms, exotic flowers and fine trees.

'But it's wonderful! Spectacular!'

It was also absolutely terrifying.

She had known that Rico was wealthy. It had been impossible to miss the evidence of the way that his money eased their path at every stage of the journey, beginning with the chauffeur-driven limousine that had picked them up from her flat and taken them to the airport, a second driver being delegated to take charge of Rico's car. Then there had been the speed with which their transit to the executive jet had been arranged, the luxurious comfort of the plane itself. But none of that had truly brought home the reality of the situation to her like this enormous, regal ranch house standing in solitary splendour in such a huge expanse of plain.

'Do you have any neighbours?' she managed to stammer, unable to take her eyes of the stunning scene.

'Not for miles—that's why we use the helicopter so much.'

Rico sounded totally relaxed, indifferent to the sheer scale of his property, but then of course he had been born and brought up here. This was 'home' to him. And he wasn't struggling to come to terms with just how isolated La Estrella was, the realisation of how totally alone she was going to be for the next week or so—alone, except for Rico.

And the passage of time had done nothing to reduce that feeling. Even the discovery that, contrary to what she had expected, Rico had arranged for her to have a separate room rather than having her installed in his master bedroom hadn't eased the stinging sense of tension that stretched her nerves tight as a violin string.

'*This* is mine?' she exclaimed, grey eyes wide with stunned bemusement as she took in what in fact amounted to a complete suite with a bedroom, bathroom and a sitting room where the wide glass-paned doors opened onto the central tiled courtyard. 'But I thought...'

'You thought that I would expect payment in kind for my hospitality?' Rico inserted when words failed her, a dark edge to his voice revealing that her comment had stung some part of his male pride, angering him deeply. 'Credit me with a little more finesse than that, *querida*. When I offered you a place to hide from the furore the cancellation of your wedding has caused, I had no ulterior motive in mind.'

Ebony eyes swept over her in such a look of disdain that it seemed to take a protective layer of skin with it, leaving her raw and vulnerable to the savage reproof in his voice.

'I—I'm sorry...' she stammered but Rico ignored her hesitant interjection, sweeping it aside with an arrogant wave of his hand.

'You needed a safe haven, somewhere to ride out the storm, and that is what I could provide. I felt I owed it to you after the part I played in ruining the plans you had for your future.'

Which was a double-edged comment if ever there was one. Felicity didn't need to be reminded of the fact that Rico believed her 'plans for the future' had involved marrying Edward simply in order to get her hands on the other man's money. In his eyes, she was nothing more than a cheap little gold-digger, one he had believed was prepared to sell herself to the highest bidder.

'Thank you.'

The sharpness of her tone betrayed her ambiguous feelings, something that didn't escape Rico's notice as she saw a spark of challenge light in the ebony eyes, making her suspect that he hadn't finished with her yet.

She was right.

'That isn't to say that I would object if you decided that you wanted to share my bed,' he drawled lazily, the gleam in his eyes growing stronger with every word he spoke. 'But that has to be your choice. You have to come of your own free will—say that you want it too.'

Which just about guaranteed that her mouth would be permanently sealed, Felicity reflected inwardly. Did he really believe that she would be able to come to him, in the clear light of day, and say quite cold-bloodedly that she wanted him? Her nerves quailed just to think of it, her stomach tying itself into tight, painful knots of tension.

'Then you'll have a very long wait if you think that's what's going to happen!' she flung at him, anger flaring up inside her as she saw one black eyebrow lift in cynical scepticism at her vehemence.

'What is it, *belleza*?' he taunted. 'Are you afraid of yourself and your feelings? Afraid to admit that you are a woman, with a woman's desires and needs?'

The challenge was overt now, leaving her with no choice but to take it up. Even to ignore it would be interpreted as backing away, and she knew that like any fierce predator Rico would pounce on any sign of weakness. If she ran, he would hunt her down, even if only mentally, and she would end up in even graver danger than when she had started.

Defiantly her chin came up, grey eyes clashing sharply with his deep-set brown ones.

'I'm afraid of nothing about my sexuality, Señor Valeron,' she told him coolly. 'Nor am I ashamed of it. It's just that I prefer to choose where and how I—indulge it. I also prefer to choose my partner for myself.'

Did she know what it did to him when those stunning eyes met his head-on like that? Rico wondered. More than likely she knew only too well, and that the provocation was deliberate. So much so that he was furious with himself for responding, for letting her get to him in the most basic, primitively erotic way possible.

He was furious with his body too. With the brutal speed with which it reacted simply to the way she looked. The blazing contrast between the sexually provocative words and the prim and proper way she spoke them made him want to reach out and haul her into his arms. He wanted to take her mouth and crush those soft lips beneath his own until he drove all thought of restraint completely from her mind.

But the suspicion that that might be exactly what she was aiming for held him back. The fight to subdue the hunger that threatened to swamp his mind, erasing all intelligence, eroded his control over his tongue, his temper slipping past his guard before he could hope to catch it back.

'You weren't so damn picky where Venables was involved,' he snarled. 'It's amazing what the promise of a wedding ring and a fortune can do to change a woman's mind—fast.'

That full, rose-coloured mouth opened on a shocked gasp of fury at the deliberate insult and her fingers itched to wipe the taunting expression from his handsome face.

'Not that it's any business of yours, but Edward and I never slept together! He never even touched me.'

'Now that I find hard to believe. For one thing, any man with a drop of red blood in his veins would be incapable of keeping his hands off you. And for another, you were definitely no virgin when you came to my bed.'

Burning colour swept up into Felicity's face then leached away again as swiftly as it had come. She was incapable of deciding whether her primary response was rage at his rudeness or a shamefaced shiver of delight at the back-handed compliment he had just dealt her.

Rage won.

'And because of that you've decided I'm some sort of tramp who'll sleep with anyone!'

'That is not what I said!'

'Near as damn it! You're a two-faced hypocrite, Rico Valeron! But, just for the record, the only man I've ever slept with was my fiancé.'

'Another one?' Rico mocked. 'Do you make a habit of collecting them and then losing them? Tell me, how many fiancés have you had in total?'

'Only one!'

Anger swirled, hot and liberating, round and round in her head like a red mist, driving away all thought of reason or control or any sense of danger. She welcomed it gladly, grateful for the way it loosened her tongue, letting the words pour out like a flood when she needed them the most.

'Only one real one, that is! Scott was my first love—my childhood sweetheart—literally the boy next door. We were both virgins, both making love for the very first time. We were going to get engaged on his nineteenth birthday but—but...'

Scalding tears were clogging her throat, choking her, but she swallowed them down, forcing herself on, wanting him to know the truth.

'He always wanted a motorbike—saved half the money for it. His mum and dad gave him the other half for his birthday and he couldn't wait to go out on it. He said he just had time to fit in one ride before the party started.'

'Felicity...' Rico tried to interject but she ignored him.

'He never came back. He took a corner too fast, skidded—right under the wheels of a bus.'

'Maldito sea!'

Rico's hands came out to hold her when she would have whirled away, unable to face him any longer.

'Felicity, I am so sorry. That was crass and insensitive of me. If I had known I never would—I never should have said anything. I behaved like a louse…'

'Yes you did!' Felicity managed between inelegant sniffs.

'If it's any consolation, I have never felt quite so ashamed of myself in my life.'

He looked it too, the coffee-coloured eyes shadowed and dull, unexpected lines of strain etched around his nose and mouth.

'I hope you will forgive me.'

It was an honest, genuine apology and, incapable of resisting the appeal in his eyes, she found herself nodding mutely, unable to deny him this.

'Did you love him very much?' His voice was unexpectedly gentle, softer than she had ever heard it before.

'At the time—yes. I thought he was the only one for me. When he died, I really believed I would never love anyone ever again. I…'

Unable to go on, she flung her hands up before her face, concealing her eyes and the expression in them from his searching gaze.

'Felicity,' Rico said again, misinterpreting the reason for her reaction. 'I'm truly sorry.'

'It's all right,' Felicity muttered, her words muffled by her concealing hands. 'Really it is—but I would like to be left alone.'

'But—'

'Rico, please!'

She risked opening her fingers, just a little bit, flashing a swift glance up at his concerned face and then away again, blinking furiously to fight back the tears.

'Please. I just want to be on my own for a bit.'

She had never seen him look so discomposed and ill at ease and it wrenched sharply at her already overwrought emotions, making her bite her bottom lip in distress.

'Please.'

For a long tense moment she thought he was going to refuse and her already bruised brain whirled in panic, trying desperately to think of some further argument she could offer to persuade him. Anything other than the truth.

'Please,' she said again, her voice wobbling revealingly.

Rico raked both hands through the black silk of his hair, expelling his breath on a long, harsh sigh that hissed through tightly clenched teeth.

'Very well,' he said roughly. 'I will leave you in peace.'

He thought she hadn't forgiven him, Felicity realised miserably. The sense of rejection and hurt pride was stamped into every stiff line of his body; it was there in his brusque movement as he stalked from the room. He believed she hadn't accepted his apology and it was all she could do not to call him back to reassure him.

But if she did that, it would not be all she would do. If she told him she forgave him, she wouldn't be able to stop there. She would have to go on, must inevitably tell him something else, something she had only just discovered for herself. Something so new and devastating that it had blasted her world into a myriad tiny pieces and she hadn't had a chance to collect them up again, never mind try to fit them back together.

'When he died, I really believed I would never love anyone ever again.'

Her own words, spoken so rashly, so intensely only a few moments before, came back to haunt her like a reproach.

She could only pray that Rico hadn't caught the momentary hesitation, the catch in her voice, that would have given away the second when her heart seemed to stop dead in shock. That he hadn't heard the break in her words as her thoughts had made her stutter, driving her to hide behind her hands, but not, as he had thought, to conceal her tears.

'I really believed I would never love anyone *ever again*.'

And in that moment she had realised just why Rico had the effect he had. Why he had hurt her so badly when he had offered her nothing but a sexual affair, which was, after all, only what Edward had offered her too.

But Edward's offer hadn't touched her emotions. She had seen his offer as an escape route, a way out of a terrible impasse, nothing more. It hadn't affected her feelings, hadn't made her *care*.

Rico made her care. He did more than make her care. He made her feel, made her hurt, made her heart sing up to the highest skies and drop down to the lowest depths of pain. And the reason why was as simple and as complicated as the reason for existing. It was all enclosed in one single, very simple word.

Love.

She loved him.

In the space of a couple of days, Rico had taken her captive physically. He had held her prisoner for his own ends, used her as a hostage in order to win whatever gains he had planned on, and by doing so he had turned her world upside down, shattering the future she had thought lay ahead of her.

But he had done so much more. He had taken her heart hostage too, and no deal, no ransom, could ever win it back for her. Even though she was no longer his prisoner but could leave whenever she pleased, she knew deep inside that she would never, ever be truly free again. Because escaping meant leaving Rico behind and if he stayed then her heart would stay with him too. And without her heart she would ever only be half the person she truly was.

CHAPTER TWELVE

'I THINK there could be thunder and lightning tonight. The atmosphere is heavy and close as if a storm is already gathering.'

Rico meant only the physical environment, Felicity reflected. He was referring to the build-up of clouds, the deepening pressure in the air. But he might as well have been talking about the emotional atmosphere between them. For days now, ever since the scene in her bedroom, the mood had been uncomfortable and tense, putting an unbearable strain on her nerves.

'A thunderstorm would certainly ease things,' she murmured, painfully conscious of the double meaning to her words. 'It's sticky and oppressive like this. Not exactly the weather for sightseeing.'

But she knew why Rico had suggested the trip into Buenos Aires. If he had come right out with it and announced that he was using the visit to Argentina's capital as a deliberate distraction and a scheme to keep them from being confined in the house together then it would have been more honest than the pretence that it was simply a sightseeing jaunt.

Honesty was something that was no longer a part of their relationship. Or, rather, the overdose of honesty that had resulted from their confrontation on her arrival at the *estancia* had driven both of them into their separate corners, away from each other. What conversation they had was stilted and awkward, overly polite. They were like two complete strangers who had only just been introduced and who didn't get on with each other at all.

Strangely enough they had communicated better when they had known each other less, she reflected. When her mind threw at her the brutally uncomfortable reminder that the sort of 'communication' she and Rico had shared within the first day of their meeting had been in the heat and hunger of her bed, she shifted uncomfortably in her seat, trying desperately to blank off her thoughts.

But her memories wouldn't be shut away. Instead they replayed over and over inside her head, bright and clear, and shockingly vivid in their sensuality. Images of kisses and caresses, of hearts beating in doublequick time, of ragged breathing and entwined, naked limbs, slick with the sweat of passion bombarded her senses until she moved restlessly on the soft leather seat, unable to escape them.

'Are you okay?' Rico had caught her uneasy movement and slanted a swift, enquiring glance in her direction.

'Fine,' Felicity managed. 'Just warm. This weather is unsettling.'

It had nothing to do with the weather. What was really unsettling her was the newly sharpened awareness of the man sitting next to her. With the remembered eroticism of her thoughts still clear in her head, she had never been so intensely aware of every tiny thing about the man who sat beside her, dark and devastating, in a black shirt and trousers, controlling the powerful car with practised ease.

If he changed gear, the muscles in his thigh bunched and flexed disturbingly. The sleeves of his shirt had been pushed back to reveal the long, bronzed forearms that tautened with every adjustment needed on the slightly bumpy road. A breeze from the partly open window tossed the silky black hair around his high forehead and blew the clean scent of his body unerringly towards her. Today he wore some faintly tangy cologne that made her think of lemons and herbs as she inhaled greedily then stopped in a flurry of embarrassment as once more she saw Rico's dark eyes slide towards her.

'What are those trees?' she covered herself by asking hastily, thankful for the fact that they were actually passing one of the clumps of dark-leaved trees that edged the road, momentarily blotting out the sun. 'The scent is familiar but I just can't place it.'

'Eucalyptus,' Rico supplied, pressing the button that controlled the electric windows to let more of the fresh scent into the car. 'It grows everywhere here. Would you like to stop somewhere and have a drink?'

'No, no, I'm fine,' she assured him hastily. 'If you really think there's a storm coming, we probably should make sure we get h—get back to La Estrella before it breaks.'

Hastily she covered her slip of the tongue, praying that Rico hadn't caught it. She had been about to say that they should get home but La Estrella would never be home to her. Her grey eyes clouded as she stared unseeingly out of the window, forcing herself to face facts.

She had fallen in love with the beautiful *estancia* as well as with its handsome owner, but it was only a temporary sanctuary, a haven where she could hide away for a short time. Very soon now she would have to leave and go back to London. She would have to face reality once again—a reality that included the terrible debts her father still owed. And with no possible way of paying them off.

'Why the deep sigh?' Once again Rico proved himself unnervingly sensitive to her mood.

'I—I was thinking about going home,' she stammered, flustered into unthinking honesty by his question. 'Do you think those reporters have grown tired of waiting by now?'

So already she was itching to get back. Rico's hands tightened on the wheel so that for a moment the knuckles of his fingers showed white under the tanned skin. He supposed it had to come some time. She had clearly been restless for the past couple of days.

'I think that after a couple of days with no activity and no sign of their quarry they have become pretty bored.'

He was quite pleased with the ruthless control that kept his answer even and indifferent in spite of the fact that his thoughts were on a totally different subject altogether.

'But if you reappear too soon then you'll only revive their interest, especially if you go back on your own.'

'Without you, you mean?'

'Yes, without the millionaire you supposedly threw your fiancé over for. Then they'll really want to know what's happening.'

What was he doing? Was he trying to convince her that she should stay? Did he really want to lay himself open to having her spurn his advances all over again? Rico berated himself. Didn't he ever learn?

Could she have made her opinion of him plainer than when she'd tossed her rejection straight into his face, declaring that she'd rather choose to be with the bloodless Edward Venables than him? And still he'd rescued her from the reporters, brought her here, in the foolish hope that if they spent some time together she might actually change her mind.

What had he said? That it had to be her choice. She had to come of her own free will—even say that she wanted it too.

Hah!

The car swerved sharply as once again his hands tightened convulsively on the wheel and he had to force himself back under control before he gave himself away completely. It would be a long, cold day in hell before this lady came to him of her own free will. And if there had been any chance of it being otherwise, then he'd trampled them into the dirt with his crass behaviour when she'd spoken of her young fiancé.

Any advantage he had earned by rescuing her from the attentions of the paparazzi had been lost then and there. Any doors that she might have opened had been slammed shut straight away and had stayed tightly closed ever since. He didn't know why he didn't just give up and let her go.

Because he couldn't. That was the simple answer. He had never felt this way about a woman before. This Felicity had wormed her way into his mind and he couldn't get her out.

'…don't you think?'

Belatedly he became aware of the fact that Felicity had spoken and, absorbed in his own thoughts, he hadn't heard her.

'*Perdón?* I'm sorry—what did you say?'

'That surely Edward would have come back by now. Won't he have explained things?'

'I doubt it. As I understand it, he has other things to occupy his mind.'

'Such as?'

'Such as his new wife.'

'His *wife*!' Felicity couldn't believe what she was hearing. 'How could that have happened?'

But Rico seemed disinclined to answer her question, instead posing one of his own.

'Tell me, *mi belleza*,' he said, apparently concentrating on negotiating a particularly uneven stretch of road. 'Were you ever going to ask me just why you're here at all?'

'I know why I'm here! The reporters… No?' she questioned as he shook his dark head.

'Before that. Didn't you ever think to wonder why I kidnapped you in the first place?'

'Hundreds of times.'

But never once had she had the nerve to ask. She'd been

too afraid of what she might have heard if she did. And as she'd come to realise what she felt about Rico that fear had grown so much worse.

'But you can't expect me to believe that if I'd questioned you about it then you'd simply have told me.'

They had arrived at the wide, wrought iron gates at the main entrance to La Estrella, heading up the long winding drive to the ranch house and Rico concentrated on the awkward turning before he answered.

'You had a right to know. You still do.'

The glance she shot him was frankly sceptical.

'You expect me to believe this?'

Rico's mouth twisted but he said nothing until they reached the top of the drive where he parked the car sharply, pulling on the brake and switching off the engine. Then he turned to face her.

'Ask,' he commanded.

Felicity swallowed hard, hunted for the words. Nothing would come. Just a single syllable.

'Why?' she croaked.

'Maria.'

It made no sense.

'Maria who? You can't mean Maria Llewellyn.'

'Who else?'

'But—what is she to you?'

Rico's lean, tanned fingers drummed for a moment on the steering wheel then stilled sharply.

'She's my sister.'

She should have known that he would never tell her the truth. Not giving the pain at his deception time to reach her, she wrenched at the door, pushed it open and scrambled out inelegantly.

'Felicity...'

Rico wasn't far behind her. Catching hold of her arm

when she would have stalked away, he swung her round to face him, looking down into her furious grey eyes.

'Oh, yes, very funny!' Felicity snapped, hating him and hating herself for the fact that it mattered so much. 'You expect me to believe that Maria *Llewellyn* who I know is very definitely Welsh is in fact the sister of Ricardo Valeron—who is very definitely not!'

'Why not?' Rico asked quietly. 'It's the truth.'

'Oh, come on…' Felicity began but then she remembered something she had learned in Buenos Aires only that afternoon.

Browsing in a bookshop, she had come across a history of Argentina and had been stunned to learn that the country had had a large number of Welsh immigrants who had stayed and founded families.

'Your *sister*?'

'Okay, my half-sister,' Rico corrected. 'My mother married Richard Llewellyn after she and my father divorced. Maria is ten years younger than me—barely twenty-one. Her father died when she was only three and our mother spoilt her rotten to compensate.'

'Edward said much the same,' Felicity managed stiffly. 'But he was less polite. "A little madam" were the words he used.'

'Yes.'

Rico's lopsided smile was dreadfully appealing, tugging sharply at Felicity's heart, but she refused to let herself weaken. As he had said, she was owed this explanation, and she wasn't going to help him give it.

'She met Edward on holiday—fell heavily for him straight away but, being Maria, she never said so. She knew he and I were business rivals—I think that added a certain piquancy to the whole thing. Maria was perfectly capable of seeing herself as one half of Romeo and Juliet with big brother cast in the role of villain if she wanted. That's probably why she didn't want to tell me she was pregnant.'

'Pregnant?' Felicity hadn't expected that. 'It was Edward's?'

Rico nodded, his expression grim.

'By then they'd quarrelled—split up. She said she wouldn't have anything more to do with him, but that was before she found out she was pregnant. She didn't tell anyone for months and, by the time she did, Venables had already announced his marriage to you.'

'It was rather a rushed arrangement,' Felicity recalled with a shiver at the way Edward had ruthlessly turned the situation to his own ends.

'The wind's getting up.' Rico had misinterpreted the reason for her reaction. 'I think the rain's on its way. We'd better go inside.'

He tried to take her arm but Felicity flinched away, unable to bear being touched. She had been nothing but a pawn to Edward, and now it seemed to Rico too. But what else had she expected? She meant nothing to him, never had and never would.

Wrapping her arms tight around her body as if to hold herself together, she marched fiercely ahead of him, unable even to look in his direction. In the large, stone-flagged hallway of the house, she stopped dead and swung round to face him.

'Are you telling me that you kidnapped me—took me hostage—for Maria's sake?'

He met her accusing eyes with amazing composure but she couldn't miss the way his sensual mouth compressed to a thin hard line before he nodded brusquely.

'Edward wouldn't listen to her—he said he was set on marrying you. I think they were both trying to score points off each other, neither of them realising how serious it had got. When it looked as if the marriage was actually going to go ahead, Maria came close to a breakdown. She was depressed, hysterical, talking about suicide. Mother begged me to help.'

'Oh, I'll just bet she did!'

It was impossible to hold the pain in any longer and it spilled out in the harsh, bitter words, the savage tone.

'And you thought that you'd do anything for little Maria. You'd march right in and screw up someone else's life instead. After all, the person involved was only some complete stranger—some silly English girl who didn't matter! Someone who for all you knew might just have been madly in love with Edward!'

That arrow had hit home. She actually saw him flinch faintly as it did do, but he recovered in an instant.

'But you weren't in love with him, were you? Maria said that was the case. She knew it wasn't going to be a proper marriage—that you were only marrying Edward for his money. She said that if I could just stop you from going to the church she was sure that she could get to Edward, persuade him to listen to her—tell him about the baby.'

'And then you'd all live happily ever after? The perfect solution!'

Felicity flung up her hands in a wild gesture that mirrored the turmoil inside her heart.

'And I suppose it never occurred to you that you could come to me—talk to me about this? Did you even try—'

'Of course I tried!' Rico snarled, eyes black with rejection of her accusation. 'I tried for days before the wedding but I couldn't reach you. You were staying at Highson House, if you remember—safe in the bosom of Edward's family. Every phone call went unanswered, every letter was returned unread.'

'Edward told me to act that way.'

For the first time Felicity's anger ebbed, leaving her feeling subdued and disturbingly vulnerable. It had never crossed her mind that Edward might have had his own personal reasons for keeping her and Rico apart at the time.

'He said it was safer because you…'

'Because I…?' Rico prompted harshly when her voice failed under a rush a realisation of the dangerous direction in which she had been heading.

Edward had told her that Ricardo Valeron was another of her father's creditors. That Joe Hamilton owed him a small fortune—and that Rico was known to be totally ruthless in taking his revenge on anyone who tried to renege on their debts.

'Just don't talk to him, don't listen to him, don't read any of his letters,' he had told her. 'As soon as we're safely married I'll settle things with Valeron and your father will be safe.'

But she couldn't tell Rico that. Not now.

When she had come to Argentina with Rico there had always been the hope, faint and weak and hidden at the back of her mind, that one day, given time to win his trust, his friendship, she might have been able to tell him the truth. That she could have admitted what her father had done and beg for some chance to put it right—paying the huge debt off in very small amounts over a very long time.

But she couldn't risk revealing that to this man. Not to this Rico who clearly felt no warmth at all towards her. This man who had used her ruthlessly once and was probably capable of doing so once again if he found out that he had cause.

'That I…?' Rico prompted again when she still hesitated. 'Felicity…'

'That you were a monster and a brute,' she flung at him in desperation as panic rushed in over her head, swamping her completely. 'A ''barely civilised savage'' was the term he used, and I think the description's pretty accurate.'

She'd hit him where it hurt that time. Right in his fierce,

male pride. She saw his arrogant head go back, his eyes
narrowing swiftly, his mouth thinning harshly.

'A monster and a brute, hmm?'

He'd forgotten that she could be like this. Forgotten the
way that she could look down that elegant nose at him,
regarding him as if he was nothing more than a nasty piece
of dirt she had picked up on her shoe. That lady of the
manor act had rubbed him up the wrong way from the
beginning and he could feel it doing so again now.

It didn't help that while she was looking at him that way,
all he could think of was how beautiful she was. With her
hair falling softly round her face, grey eyes fringed by long,
curling lashes and the sensual fullness of her mouth touched
by a rose pink gloss that made her look as if she had just
been kissed, she had a vibrant appeal that tugged at every
one of his senses. And the slim curves of her body were
shaped and enhanced by the soft blue cotton of her dress,
the scooped neckline exposing the fine lines of her neck
and throat, the short sleeves revealing long, slim arms.

'Barely civilised?'

Right now he certainly felt uncivilised. With her standing
there, head thrown back, brilliant eyes flashing fury, that
neat chin lifted defiantly, he had to fight hard with himself
not to give in to his most basic, primitive instincts.

He didn't want to argue with her. What he wanted to do
was to sweep her off her feet and carry her into the next
room, lay her on the enormous leather settee, then come
down beside her and kiss her, caress her, until they were
both senseless with passion and incapable of thought.

The mood she was in, she wouldn't go willingly. She'd
fight and scratch every inch of the way, and right now he
felt that that could only be an advantage. After three days
of just watching her move around his house, being so close
to that glorious, sexy body and not being able to touch,
after three days of frustration, waiting for her to come to

him and knowing that she was never going to, he felt like a volcano on the verge of erupting. It would only take the slightest provocation to push him from thought into action.

'When I kidnapped you, did I harm you in any way? Did I hurt you or frighten you—or even threaten you with danger? In all the time we've been together here, in this house, have you ever felt at risk, ever believed you weren't safe?'

'I...'

'Well, have you?'

'No,' Felicity admitted, unwilling to back down but knowing she couldn't lie about this. If the truth was told, even when she had felt naturally apprehensive about Rico at the start, looking back she knew that it had been the situation she was in and her own thoughts about it, not Rico's behaviour, that had made her feel that way.

'No,' she repeated.

'And have I ever laid a finger on you—except when you wanted it?'

'No...'

Her gaze dropped to the floor, embarrassed colour washing her cheeks. She couldn't look into his face and recall the times he had laid considerably more than a finger on her and she hadn't objected in the slightest.

'You kidnapped me,' she muttered ungraciously and heard his breath hiss in through his teeth in a sound of vicious impatience.

'And I've already explained why. My sister's happiness—perhaps even her life was at stake.'

Pain slashed at Felicity's heart. She would give the world to have him care for her as he obviously cared about Maria. But all she had been was a pawn in the coldly calculated game he was playing.

And making love to her. Had that been calculated too?

'Your sister! All you ever talk about is your sister! You

haven't even had the basic decency to apologise for kidnapping me.'

His laugh, hard, short, and totally mirthless, was the last thing she expected.

'Apologise,' he echoed sardonically. 'You want me to apologise for taking you away from a wedding you didn't want to go to—to a man you didn't even love?'

'I…'

She wanted to find angry words to refute his mocking question but her mind was a complete blank

'Or would you have preferred it if I had left you to marry Venables?'

And never met Rico?

'No.'

'Then I am certainly not going to apologise.'

How could he ever apologise for something that had brought this woman into his life? Even if these few days were all he was ever to have, he could never regret it, not for a second. She brightened his day by existing. She tormented him, infuriated him, drove him half out of his mind with frustration and desire, but he wouldn't have it any other way.

'I am not in the least bit sorry.'

Felicity's head came up again in a rush, the blonde mane of hair tossed back sharply.

'Oh, but I am!' she declared emphatically, lashing out blindly in her pain, wanting to hurt, as she had been hurt. 'I'm so sorry I ever met you! I can't stand even being in the same room as you! If I'd had the choice—which you weren't even courteous enough to give me—then I would very definitely have chosen marriage to Edward. I just wish you'd left me with that.'

She couldn't have said anything more guaranteed to hit him like a blow in the face. Couldn't have found any other weapon that would shatter his grip on his temper, push him over the edge of the cliff he had been struggling to keep away from.

'I wish you'd kept out of my life and left me in peace!'

'Right now, the feeling is entirely mutual!'

To his surprise, the bitterness he felt didn't show in his voice. Instead it was as cold and clipped and controlled, as if he were incapable of feeling a thing.

'But I can make things easy for you.'

That had stopped her dead, stilling the flow of angrily provocative words. She just blinked at him, a faint frown creasing the space between then fine, fair brows.

'I'm going out now—leaving you alone as you wanted. If I stay, I think we may both say things we'll regret.'

She already regretted them. Already wished them back. But it was far too late and to judge by the stony, coldly distant look that blanked off his beautiful brown eyes, she had more chance of getting through to a marble statue than she ever had of reaching him. All her anger disappeared in a rush, leaving only a bleak misery that clogged her throat, making it impossible to speak.

'If you're wise you'll use the time to get your things together and pack. When I get back I'll make the arrangements for you to get to the airport and be on your way home tonight.'

But I don't want to go home!

The words burned in her head but she couldn't get them onto her tongue. And by the time she found her voice she would have been speaking to an empty room, the door slamming to behind him the only sign that Rico had ever been there at all.

'I don't want to go home,' she said bleakly, knowing that there was no one to hear her. 'I want to stay here with you.'

CHAPTER THIRTEEN

THE storm broke immediately overhead before Rico had been gone for more than five minutes. When it did, Felicity was still standing in the huge hallway, unable to think of what to do.

She couldn't pack. She didn't want to go anywhere.

But she dreaded the prospect of Rico's return and his finding that she had ignored the order he had tossed at her as he walked out the door.

So she waited. And waited. And found herself growing more and more concerned with each minute that passed as the storm grew wilder, the rain lashing against the windows, the thunder roaring, and the lightning splitting the sky.

By the time an hour and a half had ticked by she was almost frantic with worry, her mind filled with appalling, terrifying images of Rico out somewhere in the tempest, soaked to the skin, perhaps even hurt, crushed by a branch brought down in the wind. Another half an hour with no sign of him drove her to her room to change her clothes, deciding that jeans and a white shirt would be much more practical than the light blue dress if she was forced to venture out into the downpour to find him.

She was just running back downstairs when the big main door swung open, slamming back against the wall, and Rico strode into the hall.

'You're back!'

Stupid and inane as it was, it was all she could find to say. The relief and delight at seeing him safe again made her heart leap into a frantic staccato rhythm, beating a wild song in her chest.

'You're soaked through!'

Another stupid, obvious comment. The black hair was plastered flat against his finely shaped skull, a high colour whipped into his cheeks by the whirling rain. The saturated shirt and jeans clung to the hard, lithe lines of his chest and legs in a way that was positively indecent, drying her mouth with instant desire.

She wanted to rush to him and enfold him in her arms, hug him tight, but at the same time she wanted to simply stay where she was and just look at him, absorb the full physical impact of the impressive sight. But most of all she wanted to peel off those sodden clothes and use her own body to dry and warm the rain-drenched skin beneath.

'Where have you been?'

Rico brushed a trickle of rain from his temple and raked a rough hand through the dripping strands of his hair.

'I went for a ride,' he said roughly, ebony eyes clashing with her concerned grey ones, as she stood on the stairs, a couple of steps above him.

'A ride? In this weather? Are you crazy? Something dreadful could have happened!'

'The mare is perfectly all right, *querida*, though if I'd known you would be this concerned about a horse—'

'I don't give a damn about the horse!' Felicity exploded and saw his dark brows lift in a sardonic assumption of surprise at her vehemence. 'You know perfectly well that it's you I was worried about!'

Rico's fine mouth twisted cynically, warning of the re-action she expected. He didn't disappoint her.

'I see. You wanted to make sure that I was back safe and sound in good time to get you to the airport,' he drawled with an intonation that set her teeth on edge.

'I wanted no such thing! For one thing, I'm not going home!'

'But you've changed into travelling clothes.'

'I've changed into my jeans,' Felicity told him, coming down the stairs to stand right in front of him, so close that she could see the tiny raindrops that still sparkled on the jet black eyelashes, 'because I thought I might have to go out in the storm and look for you.'

That threw him. Just for a second or two she had the intense satisfaction of seeing him look taken aback, seeing a flicker of some powerful emotion that she didn't recognise in the dark depths of his eyes. But before she had time to react, it had gone and the blank, obsidian gaze was back again.

'That's very flattering, *gatita*. But as you can see, I'm a big boy now. I can take care of myself. I don't need a nanny.'

'I'm not offering to be a nanny! Though, to be perfectly honest, you need someone to look after you!'

Exasperation and uncertainty blended in her voice. She was playing this blind, not knowing how Rico might react to anything she said, and it was frankly terrifying. If she had been walking a tightrope above a thundering waterfall she couldn't be more fearful.

'Look at you, standing there soaked to the skin. You'd better get out of those clothes and into a hot shower…'

The rest of the sentence evaporated from her mind as she saw the way he was looking at her, the brilliant eyes half-closed, gleaming behind those impossibly long lashes. He didn't need to say a word to tell her what he was thinking and she had to fight against the urge to lick her suddenly dry lips, knowing only too well the interpretation he would put on the small gesture.

'I don't suppose you'd care to join me?' he murmured softly and just for a second she was tempted.

But it was too soon. She wasn't quite ready.

'I don't think that would be a very sensible move,' she managed sharply.

'Coward.'

He didn't look back as he walked past her, didn't even glance round as he strode up the stairs.

Immediately she wished she'd had the courage to take him up on the implied challenge. Remembering how he had looked as he walked through the door, she felt the spiralling hunger that had invaded her senses then uncoiling once more deep in the pit of her stomach. From upstairs came the sound of a shower running in Rico's bathroom and before she quite knew what she was doing she had put on foot on the staircase and then another.

She was standing on the landing by the open door when he came out of the shower, his only clothing a towel fastened around his narrow waist. The contrast between the tanned skin on the lean, hard torso and the soft white cotton was almost shocking, making her lips part on a faint gasp.

He seemed totally unfazed by her appearance, black coffee eyes meeting hers head on, touched with a faint challenge. Then he simply ignored her, wandering into the room and collecting clean underwear, a white shirt, selecting black trousers from the wardrobe. He even dropped the towel and began pulling on clothes with a total lack of embarrassment.

But then, of course he had nothing to be embarrassed about. He must have known that his body was an enticement in itself. Firmly muscled, without an ounce of spare flesh on it anywhere, the broad, chest and long, long legs hazed with fine dark hair, it needed no clothes to enhance it. It was perfection in itself.

'I'm quite prepared to provide a floor show if that's what turns you on.'

Rico's dry-toned comment broke into her thoughts, sending them skittering off the erotic path they had been following.

'But I think there's something of a double standard at work here.'

'A double standard?'

She looked to Rico like a small, wild, forest creature that had been enticed to his door with handfuls of food and now was hovering in the doorway, hesitating over the decision whether to come in further or run. With her big grey eyes wide and nervous, her slender body held tensely alert, it only needed one false move and she would turn and flee and he would never get her back again.

'Yes,' he said, keeping his voice low, his tone even. 'If I was to hang around your bedroom door like that, you'd soon scream harassment—label me a voyeur, a Peeping Tom.'

No, he'd hit the wrong note there. He could see the withdrawal in her eyes, the way she took a step backwards, mentally if not physically.

'I—I'm sorry.'

'Don't be, *gatita*...'

His voice gentled, soothing her nervousness as he stepped into his trousers and pulled them up, easing the zip fastened.

'Like I said, it's fine by me. It just does beg the question—why?'

'Why?'

She looked dazed and bewildered, as if she didn't understand the question. She really didn't know what she wanted, or she was afraid of saying why she was here. He was going to have to tread carefully, take things slowly.

He reached for his shirt, slid his arms into the sleeves.

'Are you going to tell me why you're so insistent on not going home?

'I—I thought we still had some unfinished business.'

Rico considered the phrase as he slowly buttoned the shirt, leaving the neck loose and unfastened.

'What sort of unfinished business?' he asked, stamping his feet into supple black leather boots.

Now that he was dressed she found it easier to think clearly. Her thoughts could be dragged back from the wanton paths they had been pursuing, filled with images of those powerful arms around her, that bronze flesh against her own, the strong hands awakening her with burning caresses.

But the hungry ache still lingered, pulsing low down in her body and when he spoke her eyes fixed on his sensual mouth, imagining those lips on hers, the combination of hard strength and softness tantalising her senses.

'Personal business.' Her voice cracked on the words and she had to clear her throat roughly before she could go on. 'What I want…'

When had he come so close? She could have sworn that only seconds ago he had been at the other side of the room, but suddenly he was there, next to her, deep set eyes holding her own wary gaze with a mesmeric ease.

'Tell me,' he encouraged softly when she hesitated. 'Tell me what you want and if I can I'll provide it for you.'

Her lips were painfully dry and she licked them nervously, watching his dark gaze drop to follow the small movement with a disturbing intensity.

'I want to know how it might have been. I want one night with you as it would have been if we had met some other way—if you hadn't kidnapped me. I want us to start again.'

Start again. If only they could. If only it were truly possible to go back to the beginning and take a completely different path from the one they had followed. Would things have been so very different?

She had no idea. She only knew that she couldn't leave

before she had found out what it might have been like. Her first love for Scott had been snatched away from her before she had had time fully realise what it meant. The memory of some gentle kisses and caresses, a few snatched nights together, was all that she had left. But it was enough to know that, whatever she had felt for Scott, it had been nothing like this.

That had been an adolescent sort of love. A boy and girl thing. The way she felt for Rico was a fully developed, mature love. The love of a woman for a man. And even if that love was never going to be reciprocated, even if physical passion was all that Rico felt for her, for now, it was enough. It was not the sort of foundation on which to build a lifetime, but it would last through tonight. And for tonight it would be enough.

'What do you want to do?' Rico asked, his tone and his expression giving nothing away.

'What would you have done if we'd just met?' Felicity parried. 'If you'd just brought me here—as a stranger—what would we be doing?'

At least he was taking the time to consider her suggestion and not dismissing it out of hand.

'I would offer you dinner. And I would to prepare the best Argentine cuisine.'

'Wh-what would we eat?'

'My favourite—marinated lamb with roasted red pepper and peach relish served with tomato, aubergine, and basil salad…'

He was moving as he spoke, heading out of the bedroom and onto the long, wide landing. In the doorway he paused and held out his hand to her. As if in a dream, she put her own into it and let him lead her.

'You would have to taste *empanadas*—our spicy meat pastries—served with *chimichurri*, which is a sauce of herbs and garlic in oil.'

He was taking her down the other corridor, away from the stairs, and automatically Felicity went with him, walking at his side, their steps matching exactly, the softly accented sound of his voice swirling round her like scented smoke, weaving a spell of delight.

'We would drink the finest Malbec wine, and for dessert—what else but *dulce de leche* with melon and figs?'

'My mouth is watering already.' Felicity knew a twist of disappointment as they reached a polished wood door at the end of the corridor and he pushed it wide open.

But Rico did not release her as she had anticipated; instead he gave the hand he held a gentle tug that whirled her in a half circle until she was standing face to face with him, grey eyes locking with deepest brown, their bodies lightly touching at breast and hips and thigh.

'A-and when we'd eaten, then what would we do?'

She was trembling all over but not from fear. Her reaction came from the sharpest, most intensely heightened awareness of all that made up this man before her. The heat of his hand against hers, the controlled strength in the fingers curled around her own. The clean, fresh scent of his freshly washed skin enfolded her in its own embrace, and the jet-black hair was still crisp and damp from the shower.

'Then...'

Rico's voice had dropped an octave or more, becoming a husky whisper that curled her toes inside her shoes.

'Then, *mi belleza*, we would dance. And in Argentina there is only one dance.'

'Of course,' she breathed. 'The tango.'

Only that afternoon, in the Plaza Dorrego in Buenos Aires, she had watched the tango dancers arch and twist and sway in the open air. And in the Chacarita cemetery there had been the life-size bronze statue of Carlos Gardel, the most famous of all tango singers, in his tuxedo, with his hair slicked back, and with bunches of red flowers at his feet, or stuck in the crook of his arm, by his ardent fans.

'I'm afraid I'm not exactly dressed for dancing.'

Her smile was tremulous, her laughter a nervous bubble in her throat as she looked down at her shirt and jeans, her practical trainers.

'Something that is easily remedied.'

Rico swung her round again, this time until she was facing into the room. On the opposite wall hung an oil painting of a woman, dark-haired and dark-eyed, wearing a deep red, traditional Spanish flamenco dress.

'Who is she?' she managed to ask, her heart thudding in response to the way that his arms held her, coming round her ribcage, and crossing over her breasts, his long-fingered hands resting lightly on her shoulders, only inches away from the spot where an urgent pulse throbbed at the base of her throat.

'My grandmother.'

Of course. She could see the resemblance in the eyes, the high cheekbones.

'She's beautiful—and so is the dress.'

'I still have it.'

Gently he led her over to a carved wooden chest. When he flung back the lid the fragrant scent of sandalwood filled the air. Rico lifted out a rustling package, carefully wrapped in tissue paper, slid it on the bed and opened it delicately. The fine silk of the dress spilled out onto the white bed cover.

'Rico…' It was a sigh of delight.

'My grandmother was about your size.' He picked up the dress, held it up against her, nodding his dark head in satisfaction. 'From the moment that I brought you here I have had a fantasy of seeing you in it.'

He stroked the back of one hand against her cheek then

slid it under her chin, lifting her face so that her eyes met the darkness of his.

'Indulge me, *querida*,' he murmured softly. 'Put it on.'

When he looked at her like that, spoke to her like that, she could deny him nothing. She nodded silently and he put the dress into her hands where she barely even noticed she was holding anything, the silk was so delicate and fine.

'I'll be downstairs,' he said and bushed her cheek with his lips, leaving a burning trail of promise.

He was waiting for her at the foot of the great wooden staircase when she appeared, smiling a little nervously, yet with a glow of feminine pride about her. Her mirror had told her that she looked good, but Rico's eyes told her more than that. They watched her every step of the way down the stairs and the unmoving, dark-eyed gaze told her that she was beautiful without a single word having to be spoken.

But he found the words too, coming to her as she reached the last step and holding his hand out to her and clasping hers firmly as she came to stand level with him.

'You are perfection, *querida*,' he told her in a voice husky with deep sincerity. 'You have never looked more lovely, and if my grandmother could see you now she would be happy to have that dress worn by someone who enhances it the way you do.'

He had known that she would look stunning, but he hadn't been prepared for quite how spectacular her appearance was. The deep red of the dress looked amazing against the pale gold of her skin, the sleeveless design and low-cut vee neckline exposing delicate arms and just a hint of the sweetly feminine curves of her breasts.

Tightly-fitting to the waist, the dress then flared out into a full-length skirt, slit right up the centre with wide flounces one either side, exposing long slender legs, almost to the hip. She wore delicate black sandals with ridiculously high heels that accentuated the length of her limbs even more, tilting her body forward so that he had to drag his hungry eyes away from the creamy cleavage so blatantly on display.

But he couldn't just stand and stare, however much he wanted to. She had asked for one night and if that was all he could give her he would make sure it was a night to remember. So he took her hand and led her, out of the hallway, through the long living room, and out on to the veranda where the wine bottle and glasses stood ready on the wooden table.

'I don't have the food yet, but I do have wine. Can I pour you a glass?'

'Please.'

It was only now that Felicity realised that the storm had stopped its crashing and growling. The lightning no longer flashed and there was an atmosphere of intense calm all around them. The rain washed grass looked fresh and deeply green, with tiny droplets of water still sparkling here and there like miniature diamonds and far away on the clear horizon the faint outline of the high Andes could just be seen.

Their hands touched faintly as he passed her the glass and it seemed as if hot shivers of electricity ran up her arm underneath her skin and suffused her whole body. She jumped faintly as if she had been burned then wished she hadn't as she saw his immediate withdrawal.

'And the music?' she asked, anxious to repair the damage. 'Did you find some tango music?'

'Of course.'

He moved inside for a moment and she heard the faint click of a CD case opening and being placed into a machine. A few seconds later the first, delicate strains of sound drifted out on to the veranda.

It seemed as if the music went straight to her heart with

its plaintive surface layer of the *bandoneon*—the big, black concertina—and its heavier, sensual undercurrents of guitar and rhythm. She felt tears burn in her eyes and hastily bent her head to sip at some wine as she struggled with her feelings.

'Would you like to dance?' Rico was suddenly there beside her, his footsteps light as a cat's, unheard even on the wooden floor.

'I—I don't know how.'

'Then I will teach you.'

Gently he took the wineglass from her unresisting hands and laid it on the table. Then he moved her so that she was standing in front of him, a few inches away, her arms hanging loosely at her sides.

'Your arms go here…'

He lifted her left hand and placed it low down on his right shoulder, almost at the top of his arm.

'And here…'

He linked hard tanned fingers of his left hand with the paler, slender ones of her right and, looking down into her eyes, smiled suddenly, devastatingly.

'The tango always had the reputation of being immoral and sinful. Until late in this century, no respectable woman would take part in such a dance because it was reputed to have started in the brothels…and one of the reasons for that is that a man can hold his partner like this…'

His free hand slid around her waist, drawing her close and holding her tight so that there was barely enough space to let a shaft of light in between their two bodies. The palm of his hand was in the small of her back where the low-cut back left her skin exposed, the light touch seeming to burn like a brand.

'Now listen to the rhythm… Played by true *tangueros*, tango music is dark, dangerous. To dance to it you have to let it take over your body, enter your soul…'

Felicity heard his words only vaguely through the pounding in her head. It was a pulse that had nothing to do with the music that surrounded them, and everything to do with the man who held her, his lean hard body so very close to her own. She didn't so much follow the rhythm of the accordion and guitar as blindly match the sinuous slide and twist and turn of the long legs, the supple hips, the proud, straight back of her partner.

And she had no idea how she managed to dance when she was totally unaware of her feet. When all her being, all her soul was concentrated in her eyes as they locked with the ebony deep gaze just inches above her, burning, sensual, demanding, like the music.

They danced slowly at first, then picked up speed, stepping, turning, sliding, twisting, dipping, until her head was whirling and her body on fire. He spun her away from her, then back again with only a slight, arrogant twist to his wrist; he bent her backwards, leaning low from the waist with only the hard strength of his arm supporting her in the small of her back. He held her close, with his cheek resting against hers, his warm breath softly stirring the tendrils of her hair with a gentleness that tore at her already vulnerable heart.

And as the last bars of the music died away he caught her to him and his lips came down hard on hers, all the fire and beauty of the dance compressed into one searing, demanding kiss.

A kiss that she answered with all her heart. She lifted her head and opened her mouth to him in the same seconds that her arms went up around his neck, fingers clenching in the black silk of his hair as she held him close. Her hunger was a tango beat in her blood, running molten through her veins, melting away all thought but one.

'Rico,' she muttered against his mouth, her voice husky with need. 'You said I had to come to you of my own free

will. That I had to be the one to say I wanted you that I…
Well, I'm saying it now. I want you, Rico. I want you more
than I can say. I…'

But she didn't have to say any more because even before
she had framed half her words Rico had reacted to the tone
of them, the yearning hunger that made her voice crack in
the middle. While she was still speaking he swung her off
her feet and up into his arms, carrying her into the house,
kicking doors open in his impatience.

Her carried her up the wide, wooden staircase, across the
landing and along the corridor to his bedroom where he
laid her gently on the bed then stood back slightly, bending
to cup her face in both hands and stare down into her eyes,
his burning gaze seeming to reach right into her soul.

'I have waited so long for this, *querida*,' he muttered,
his words thick and rough with a need that matched hers.
'It may only have been days in time but each hour, each
second since I first made love to you has seemed like an
eternity to me. To watch you and want you and not be able
to touch…'

He broke off, shaking his proud dark head in despair at
his memories.

'But now the waiting is over. For both of us. And I
promise you—I promise you, *gatita*—that I will make this
well worth waiting for.'

Her body was already aroused and hungry, her skin on
fire for his touch. It was as if the dance they had shared
had been the most provocative, the most erotic form of
foreplay so that already the need was at its highest pitch,
the pleasure so sharp it was close to pain.

But still he prolonged the waiting, taking his time to ease
the clinging dress from her body, to dispense with the
scraps of lace and satin that were her only covering underneath it. He kissed, caressed, sucked, licked every inch of
her skin until she was writhing beneath his tormenting

hands, pressing herself against the hot demand of his lips. Her breathing was ragged and uneven, his name a litany of praise on her lips.

And she gave him back kiss for kiss, caress for caress. She tugged the buttons on his clothing free, a sigh of delight escaping her as she eased the white shirt from his shoulders and down his back. But then with the sleeves halfway down his back, the white material stretched tight, imprisoning him, she paused and smiled up into his passion-glazed eyes, her expression teasingly provocative.

'My turn now…' she murmured and she twisted out from under him, pushing him down onto the soft sheets where the tanned skin glowed like burnished gold in contrast to the pristine whiteness surrounding him.

Felicity bent her head and set herself to reducing this proud, forceful man to the same state of agonised, quivering yearning, to arousing the same white-hot hunger that he had created in her. She traced the line of every taut muscle in his chest, with lingering kisses, smiling against his skin as she felt them bunch and clench under her mouth. She let her tongue encircle the tight bud of his male nipple, until it peaked against her mouth, his groan a sound of aching delight and pure surrender all rolled into one.

Leaving the shirt where it was, still restricting his movement, she slid lower down his long, hot body, taking the same, slow, deliberate time to unfasten his belt, ease, down the zip, smooth his clothes the length of his legs and onto the floor. And then, as he had done the first time they had made love, she kissed her way upwards again, hearing his breath catch thickly in his throat as her lips brushed the heated hardness of his potent desire for her.

'Felicity… *gatita*…!'

She had suspected all along that the imprisonment of his shirt was not enough to hold him, but that he had simply been going along with her love play, content to submit completely to her attentions. But it was clear that even his iron grip on his control was loosening and she was only allowed a few more seconds of freedom to torment him before with a hoarse cry of hunger he wrenched his arms free, ripping the shirt to pieces in a second, and reared up to capture her again.

She was flung down onto her back, her limbs imprisoned and crushed by the hard strength of his, one of his knees coming between her legs, a hard thigh nudging hers apart.

'Now...' he muttered thickly, ebony eyes glittering wildly, a hot streak of colour burning high on the carved cheekbones. 'Now I will show you what I really feel.'

She was already open to him. Already lifting her pelvis to meet the wild, fierce thrust of his body, welcoming him inside her with a sense of such glorious inevitability that she almost lost herself right there and then. But Rico wasn't prepared to let her rush to fulfilment and he stilled for a moment, gentled her with soft kisses and butterfly caresses. And only when her frantic breathing had slowed faintly, when her closed eyelids began to flutter open, did he move again.

And this time there was no going back. This time neither of them had a hope of imposing any sort of control over their actions. Their loving was wild and fast and hard and everything she needed. It was elemental and overpowering and it carried her along with the force of a raging floodtide, on and on and up and up until in one final peak of ecstasy she was catapulted into the stars and her whole being exploded within her.

She didn't know whether she slept for a time or whether she simply lost herself so completely that the time slid away without her realising it. She only knew that when a faint, hazy form of consciousness returned, she was lying curled up against Rico's long, muscular body, the warm, heavy weight of his arm imprisoning her, her head on his shoulder, cheek resting against the heated satin of his skin.

As she lay there listening to the heavy, rhythmic thud of his heart, which was the only sound in the darkness of the night, she found that one persistent nagging question slid into her mind and wouldn't leave, no matter how hard she tried to force it away.

Had tonight been the start of something wonderful or merely the wild, passionate ending to all that she and Rico had shared?

She didn't know and no matter how hard she tried no answer would come until she was too tired to think any more. And because she was very much afraid that an ending was what it was, a single desolate tear slid from her eye and down onto Rico's chest as sleep claimed her once again.

CHAPTER FOURTEEN

THE fax came through early in the morning.

Lying in bed, warm, relaxed and indolently lazy, with Felicity's softly perfumed body curled up next to him, Rico was at first thoroughly disinclined to do anything about it.

He knew what it was. He had asked the manager of one of his companies to send him through the details of a problem they had been having with their finances. It seemed someone had been embezzling large amounts for some time, salting them away in a variety of neatly inconspicuous ways that had meant the perpetrator was exceptionally hard to trace. A report at this time of the day, allowing for the time difference in England, could only mean one thing. They had tracked down the guilty person.

He supposed he really should go and check it out. He could be down there, assess the situation, fax the necessary instructions for the inevitable prosecution and be back in bed before Felicity even stirred.

Which was exactly how he wanted it, he thought, dropping a soft kiss on her sleep-warmed cheek. He had very special plans for the moment that she woke—and once they'd made love again he was going to ask her to marry him. If last night had taught him anything, it was that there was no way he could spend the rest of his days without this woman in his life.

'Sleep on, *gatita*,' he whispered as after pulling on jeans and a light blue tee-shirt, he returned to kiss her once more. 'I won't be more than a few minutes.'

When she sighed and murmured in her sleep he very nearly abandoned the idea and got back into bed with her.

But he was up now, and dressed. He might as well get it done.

The report was longer than he had anticipated. And as he read it his mood changed completely, all the lazy good humour vanishing to be replaced by shock, disbelief, and a black wave of fury that swamped every other thought in his head.

'Joe Hamilton...' he muttered savagely, his hand clenching brutally on the paper he held. 'Damn him to hell—and his conniving, deceiving, *lying* daughter with him!'

It was at that moment that the door was pushed slowly open and Felicity stood, still blinking sleepily, on the doorstep.

She had clearly only just got out of bed and her hair was wildly tousled—by his hands, he thought on a rush of anger, refusing to let himself remember how those soft golden strands had felt under his touch. Her cheeks were still faintly flushed and she had pulled on the nearest thing to hand—a white towelling robe—*his* white towelling robe that swamped her slim form, even though she had belted it tightly around her slender waist.

He only fully realised just *how* angry he was when he understood how his body, only too urgently receptive to just the sight and thought of her during the night, remained stubbornly unresponsive as she wandered into the room.

'Good morning, *querida*,' he managed cynically, biting off the words with a snap.

There was something wrong here, Felicity thought—very wrong. She had woken just a few minutes ago as Rico left the room. At first she had planned to wait until he came back to bed but as the time ticked away had grown impatient for the feel of his arms around her, the touch of his lips on hers. And so she had pulled on his robe and followed him, eagerly anticipating how glad he would be to see her.

But 'glad' described a position light years away from the one that Rico had taken up. His dark eyes were black with rejection, his beautiful mouth clamped into an ugly line, and the intonation on that *'querida'* had turned it into a scathing insult and not the gentle term of affection she was used to.

'Rico? What's wrong?'

Oh, but she was good! If he didn't have the proof to the contrary in his hands, he would have believed that she actually meant what she had said. That she didn't even suspect...

But of course, she didn't know that the fax he held was the evidence of her corruption. The end of her little scheme. The fact that it was also the end of those all too briefly acknowledged dreams of a future with her that he had just allowed himself to consider made his tone savage as he rounded on her.

'What's wrong? *Por Dios—this—this* is what's wrong!'

Felicity stared blankly at the paper he thrust at her, not understanding. But then when he crammed it into her hands, his dark scowl looking positively murderous, she had no alternative but to take it from him and try to read it.

At first the letter blurred and danced before her eyes but finally she forced herself to focus and immediately wished that she hadn't.

'Oh.'

'Oh!' he echoed with suppressed violence, the scathing note in his voice flaying off a protective layer of skin and leaving her nerves exposed and vulnerable. '*Oh*. Is that all you can say?'

'What else would you want me to say?' Pain made her voice high and sharp. 'That it isn't true?'

He would be fool enough to believe her if she did. He would believe it because he wanted to. Because he wanted her to have nothing to do with this. If she had known, then how would he ever be able to convince himself that she had gone to bed with him because she cared and not just as the next stage in whatever malicious little scheme she had cooked up with her father?

'Is it true?'

'Yes.'

It was just a thin thread of sound, too weak to be clear even though he was so very close.

'What?'

'I said, *yes*! Yes it's true. Yes, my father got into debt; and yes, he took your money; and yes, I was going to marry Edward because he promised me if I did that he would make sure the money was paid back and you never found out.'

His head went back sharply, his eyes growing even darker. He hadn't even thought about that. He'd forgotten—he'd actually *forgotten*—that she had been about to marry Edward Venables.

He'd never known a pain like it. The sense of betrayal was like acid in his guts, eating away at him savagely. Only that morning, in the long, silent hours before dawn, he'd come to realise how much this woman meant to him. He'd admitted to himself that he loved her—the first time he had ever used that word about any female he'd been involved with. If the fax had come through just an hour or so later he would actually have told her...asked her...

'But I did find out, *gatita*,' he snarled. 'I found out and now all your scheming, all your lying, was for nothing. You even made the ultimate sacrifice and went to bed with me—to no avail.'

'The ultimate...'

The words knotted in her throat, choking off the rest of the sentence.

'Oh, no! No! No!'

'Oh, come now, *querida*, please.'

His derision was harder to take than his anger as he leaned back against the side of the desk, black eyes mocking her cruelly.

'Don't tell me that you're still trying to stick to your story of last night. That you're still claiming you wanted me for myself.'

'But I did! I did!'

She flung the words into his set, stony face, anguish tearing at her heart as she saw the way that not even a flicker of movement betrayed any sort of feeling. He was closed off from her completely, shutting her out, and she could pound on the barriers he had built up around him until her hands were raw and bleeding and there would never be any response.

'Spare me the pretence,' he scorned. 'I may have swallowed it last night, but this morning the blinkers have very definitely gone from my eyes. I can see you for what you really are and, believe me, I don't like what I find.'

'Do you really think—?'

'I don't think—I know,' Rico shot back. 'I know that you're a liar and a cheat and that you and your father are two of a kind. So tell me, *gatita*...'

His use of the once gentle word made her bare toes curl in horror on the polished wooden floor.

'All those nights you spent in that nightclub—was that your own money you were wasting or—'

'Nightclub?' Felicity broke in sharply. 'I don't know what you're talking about! What nightclub?'

'The Top Hat, I believe it was called. You were seen— I had someone watching you.'

'You...'

Her head spun with the horror of it all, the bitter realisation that he actually believed...

'Then you were wrongly informed! Your detective or

whoever you employed clearly didn't do their job properly because if they had they would have known that I wasn't enjoying myself in that place! I wasn't spending your money or anyone's money—I was earning it! I was working there, damn you!'

'But you already had a job...'

'But not one that earned enough to go any way towards paying back what my father owed! What he'd stolen from you!'

He hadn't expected that; it was there in the stunned look to those beautiful dark eyes. She couldn't even begin to guess if he believed her or not but she was past caring. If she had ever been fool enough to believe that there might be a chance of a future for herself and Rico, then she knew now that that dream had been nothing but an illusion. It had died, shrivelling to nothing in her wounded heart, when she had looked into his eyes and seen nothing there but black disgust and total rejection.

'Oh, I know that what I earned could have been nothing more than a drop in the ocean of debts that Dad owed but I had to do something! I still do. Rico—please...'

She couldn't stop herself from coming forwards, taking hold of his hands, her bruised-looking grey eyes pleading with him to listen to her, even though she knew she was risking the sort of rejection that would tear her heart in two.

'Please, just give me a chance—give me time. My father has—had—a gambling problem. It got him into terrible debt and the only way out of that debt that he could see was one that made matters even worse. But he knows what he's done is wrong and he's going to try—he's seeing an addiction counsellor and I'm sure he's on the road to recovery. I'll do anything I can—everything I can...'

The words died on her lips as Rico shook off her clinging hands with a cold disdain, straightening up and walking to the window. With his shoulders hunched and his hands pushed deep into the pockets of his jeans, he stared out, seeing nothing, for a long, long moment. Then at last he turned.

'Anything?' he questioned harshly and the coldness of his eyes, the carefully blanked off expression sent a shiver crawling down Felicity's spine.

'A-anything,' she managed apprehensively.

To her astonishment he actually smiled. But the smile was far worse than the coldness, the harsh rejection of only moments before.

'Well, then, we don't have a problem.'

'We—we don't?'

'No, we don't.'

Coming back to the desk, he rested both hands flat on its polished surface, leaning forwards to look straight into her face. Felicity had to fight hard against the desire to flinch away from that brutally glacial, emotionless survey that swept over her from the top of her blonde head to where her small, bare feet rested on the polished floor.

'I think I have a solution that will suit us both.'

A solution. It was what she desperately needed, so why did it not sound right? Why did those words that should have lifted her heart, made it sing in hope and relief, instead weigh her down more than ever, threatening to drag her deep into a bottomless pit of despair?

'What sort of solution?'

If only she didn't have to look at him. If only she could close her eyes tight so that she didn't have to be so painfully aware of the hard masculine beauty of his face, the brilliance of his eyes, the softness of the glossy black hair. If only she could blot out the awareness of the forceful physical impact of his long, lithe body, the hard strength of muscle in the taut arms that supported him, the trim waist and hips, the powerful length of leg in the close-fitting denims.

As always, her sensual response to him scrambled her thoughts, muddling and confusing her just when she most needed to be able to concentrate and think clearly.

'The solution where we all get exactly what we want. Not quite *how* we wanted it, perhaps, but that would be perfection and perfection is impossible to attain.'

Felicity shook her head in bewilderment.

'I don't understand.'

'Marry me.'

The words were like a slap in the face, stopping her dead and making what little colour she had left leach from her skin leaving her ashen and drained, her eyes looking like two dark bruises about her pale cheeks.

'Marry…'

There was that travesty of a smile again and it was so much worse this time.

'There's something in it for all of us. You get the rich husband you were after from the start—a far wealthier one than ever Venables could have been. You get your father's debts paid off, making him safe from prosecution…'

'And you?'

'Isn't it obvious, *mi ángel*? I get you in my bed every night.'

Misery tasted sour in Felicity's mouth. She couldn't swallow it down for fear she would actually be physically sick and so she could only shake her head in silent despair at what he was suggesting.

'No?' Rico questioned sceptically. 'You're actually turning me down?'

'I won't even give your suggestion the honour of considering it!' Felicity flung at him, pain forcing her to speak at last. 'I don't know how you could even believe I would. I could never marry you under those conditions!'

'Why not? You were prepared to marry Edward.'

'Yes, but…'

Yes, but I didn't love Edward.

Horrified at what she had been about to reveal, she caught herself up hastily.

'But I—I couldn't think of anything else to do.'

'And you can now?'

'No… But you can't…'

'But I *can*.'

'You'd marry me and pay all that money—just to—wouldn't a whore be cheaper?'

His glare was savage, searing over her skin.

'I don't do cheap! I only want the best.'

'And the best is me?' Frank incredulity rang in her voice.

'Don't put yourself down, *querida*. If last night taught me anything it's that you're very definitely the best. Edward doesn't know what he's missing.'

'I wouldn't have been like that with Edward.' The words escaped before she'd had a chance to consider whether they were wise. 'In fact I very much doubt that I could have gone through with that marriage if I hadn't been doing it for Mum.'

Realising belatedly just what she had said, she clamped her hands over her mouth as if to hold the words back but it was already far too late.

'Your mother?' Rico asked sharply, straightening up. 'And what has your mother to do with all this? Did she know what was going on?'

'No! She knew nothing about it. She still doesn't. The one thing that is to my father's credit is that he hid everything from her—never let her even suspect that anything was wrong. You see, she's not well—she has a weak heart. The doctor said she's not to be stressed, not to be worried. Any sort of problem could—if she has another attack, she could…'

She couldn't say the word, couldn't force her tongue to frame it. But she knew she didn't have to. Rico knew what she meant without any further explanation being necessary. The look of understanding he gave her told her that and she was grateful for it. It brought a faint amount of warmth to ease some of the ice that seemed to have enclosed her heart. And it gave her the strength to carry on.

'That's why I couldn't see my father go to jail. Oh, I've no doubt he deserves it for what he's done, but it would hurt my mother so terribly. I don't think she'd ever recover.'

'And Edward knew about this?'

Felicity's nod was slow, her expression forlorn.

'He knew.'

'And used it to his advantage—the bastard!'

Rico's voice was rough and uneven, echoing the turmoil in his conscience. If he hated the thought of the way Venables had behaved, how could he paint himself as snow white in all this? Wasn't he just as bad as the other man?

And Felicity? What did he think of Felicity? He didn't know; that was the truth of it. His mind seemed to veer back and forth from loving to hating and back again. And yet, deep down, he knew that the hate was only because he loved her so much that she could hurt him, and so it was really one and the same thing all the time.

'So—my proposal...' he managed huskily. 'What is your answer?'

Felicity bit down sharply on her lower lip to hold back the cry of pain that almost escaped her. This was going to be so very, very hard. But it had to be done.

'My answer is no,' she managed and surprised herself with the steadiness of her words, the conviction in her tone. 'It can't be anything else.'

'But your mother—your father...'

'I hope they'll understand. I'll be there to help them as much as I can. Perhaps if you could give us more time, we can do something about paying you back. But I can't let you do this, Rico. You don't really want to marry me and I can't ask it of you. It's too much.'

She was turning away as she spoke. In another second she would walk out the door and he would have lost her completely.

'I'll forget the whole thing—write off the debt—no prosecution—no strings.'

'What?'

It brought her spinning round, shock, frank confusion and total disbelief written all over her face.

'Rico—you don't mean that? Why would you do that?'

'I can afford it.'

Something about his tone, a strangely defensive look in his eyes, a tautness of the muscles in his jaw gave away the fact that his throwaway tone wasn't in the least bit genuine. And if she looked closer she could see the white lines of strain etched around his nose and mouth, feathering out from his eyes.

'I know you can afford it,' she said carefully, feeling her way blindly through this sudden, inexplicable change in atmosphere. 'But why would you do it and get nothing in return? It doesn't make sense. It's crazy.'

'Love makes fools of us all.'

'What?'

Could she believe what she had heard?

'Rico…'

He threw his hands out in an expressive gesture of defeat, the twist to his mouth wry and self-mocking.

'Yes, I said love,' he declared with a touch of bravado. 'I said love and meant love. And if that makes me a fool then I don't give a damn. I love you more than my life, more than my self-respect, and I would do anything to keep you with me.'

Felicity's heart was soaring, setting the blood singing through her veins. Rico had spoken the words that she had

only ever heard in her dreams and had never believed that
she would ever hear in real life. He had said that he loved
her.

'If being in love makes you a fool,' she said softly but
urgently, needing him to hear it, 'then I'm every bit as big
a fool as you. Because I love you too, Rico. I'm crazy about
you—out of my mind with love for you.'

His expression brought tears of delight to her eyes. His
face was a perfect blend of stunned confusion and burning
delight. And the blazing light that warmed the darkness of
his eyes melted away any last lingering doubts she might
have, leaving her totally sure that he felt the same way too.

'*Por Dios, gatita*, come here and let me hold you.'

She flew into his outstretched arms, felt them come
round her, enfolding her, gathering her close, and it was
like coming home at the end of a long, miserable journey.

Rico's kisses were everywhere. On her hair, her temples,
her cheeks, the closed eyelids, and then at last, long and
lingering and totally loving, on her mouth. And if there
were any doubts or questions left that kiss asked and answered them all at once. Felicity's heart was flooded with
the sort of deep, burning peace and contentment that she
had never known before. It was a wonderful, glorious, totally overwhelming experience and one that every instinct
told her she would know every day for the rest of her life
with Rico.

'But you said you wouldn't marry me,' Rico muttered
roughly when at last they were forced apart by the need to
breathe.

'I couldn't have lived with you and never shown my
love,' Felicity told him, losing herself in the deep pools of
his eyes. 'And when I thought you didn't love me, I knew
I couldn't go through with it, even to rescue my dad. And
besides, I couldn't do it to you. You deserved so much

better. You needed a wife you could love, a wife who would love you…'

'And now I've found her. I've found more than a wife, I've found a soulmate, someone I'll be proud to have at my side now and all the days of my future—if you'll have me, *querida*.'

'Of course I'll have you,' Felicity sighed her happiness. 'I couldn't want any other man after I'd met you. You are my future too—my love, my happiness and my life.'

'And you're mine,' Rico declared with husky sincerity as his mouth came down on hers.

The car pulled up outside the house and Rico pushed open the door, getting out hastily, then turning back into the vehicle, holding out his hand to Felicity who sat on the back seat, still dressed in the ivory satin and lace of her wedding dress.

'We're here, *querida*,' he said softly. 'We're home.'

Home. Felicity savoured the word as she slid from the car to stand at her new husband's side, leaning against him slightly as she contemplated the elegant house before her.

It seemed impossible now to remember how it had felt when she had first seen this house, on the day that Rico had abducted her and brought her there. Everything had changed so much that it didn't seem possible it had only been a month before.

'Happy?' Rico whispered and she could only nod silently, too full of joy to speak.

'Happy doesn't describe the way I'm feeling,' he told her. 'I'm the most ecstatic man on the planet. I can't put my emotions into words.'

He didn't have to, Felicity reflected. His joy was there in his smile, in the light in his eyes, the lilt in his voice.

'It was a wonderful wedding, wasn't it? Everyone seemed to enjoy themselves—even Edward.'

'Maria and Edward will settle down,' Felicity reassured him. 'She's so very young—and they're both going to have to learn the world doesn't begin and end with them—but from everything Edward told me I think he truly does love Maria and he'll try to make her happy.'

'As I will you.'

'You don't have to try. You've already made me the happiest person alive when you made me your wife.'

Looking up into Rico's warm, dark eyes she chuckled in amusement at a memory.

'I think everyone thought we were crazy, not even waiting to change before we left the reception.'

'They didn't know we had a special little ceremony we had to perform for ourselves. Ready?'

She nodded smilingly and he reached out, swept her off her feet and lifted her up into his arms.

'We've done this once before, *mi ángel*,' he told her. 'But this time it's for real.'

And he carried her over the threshold of the home they would share, up the wide staircase and into their bedroom, kicking the door firmly closed behind them.

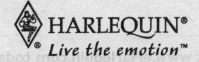

If you enjoyed what you just read,
then we've got an offer you can't resist!

Take 2 bestselling love stories FREE!

Plus get a FREE surprise gift!

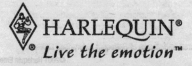

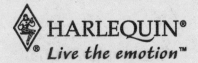